# Lucinda Sly

Irish edition published in 2008 by Coiscéim
English translation published in 2013 by
Liberties Press
140 Terenure Road North | Terenure | Dublin 6W
Tel: +353 (1) 405 5701
www.libertiespress.com | info@libertiespress.com

Trade enquiries to Gill & Macmillan Distribution
Hume Avenue | Park West | Dublin 12
T: +353 (1) 500 9534 | F: +353 (1) 500 9595 | E: sales@gillmacmillan.ie

Distributed in the UK by
Turnaround Publisher Services
Unit 3 | Olympia Trading Estate | Coburg Road | London N22 6TZ
T: +44 (0) 20 8829 3000 | E: orders@turnaround-uk.com

Distributed in the United States by
Dufour Editions | PO Box 7 | Chester Springs | Pennsylvania 19425

ISBN: 978-1-907593-58-1
2 4 6 8 10 9 7 5 3 1

A CIP record for this title is available from the British Library.

Printed and bound by Bell & Bain Ltd., Glasgow

Urraithe ag

Foras na Gaeilge

The publishers acknowledge the financial support of Foras na
Gaeilge in relation to the translation costs associated with this
project.

# Lucinda Sly

## A Woman Hanged

Maidhc Dainín Ó Sé

Translated from the Irish by Gabriel Fitzmaurice

# On My Rambles, 2006

It was on a fine day in April that I travelled the long road from my home in Kerry to Carlow town. I had a fortnight's work ahead of me there and I was eager to find out about these people who lived closer to the east coast than I did.

I arrived in Carlow early on a Sunday evening. After I had secured lodgings and taken a shower, I went for a walk around the town. I knew little about the town itself but that was quickly going to change. There was a fine long evening ahead of me and it was too early to put my backside on a bar stool.

I walked the town from top to bottom and from side to side. It was a wide, sweeping town with buildings new and old. Even though it was Sunday, the traffic on the streets was reasonably heavy. When I was going to school I learned that Carlow was a county of mixed religions. Without a doubt, the British influence was still strong throughout the county and had survived from generation to generation. Remember that this was a garrison town for a long time until the British were chased out of it. I remember having heard that there was a sugar factory there until recently. This allowed the local farmers to grow sugar beet and transport it to the factory at little cost.

The land was also suitable for fattening dry stock. Often buyers would come to West Kerry to purchase yearling calves or two-year-old heifers for fattening on the rich land of Carlow having left our poor fields.

But it isn't to give an account of the fertile land in Carlow that I put pen to paper here but to tell a true story – a piteous tale of a tragedy you wouldn't wish on enemy or friend. It wasn't in search of a subject that I made the long journey to Carlow. No! But rather, as I would in any town in Ireland, to find out what kept, and keeps, the heart of the town beating.

Having completed my walk, I saw a seat in front of me that looked like it was for public use. I was sweating profusely as I hadn't done a walk like that for some time. Exhausted, I sat down, stretched against the back of the seat and spread my legs across the bottom rung. I looked around. I saw nothing I hadn't seen in any big town in Ireland. Pedestrians passed me, some over and some back. Two saluted me, three didn't. Then a few minutes with not a Christian passing by.

I wasn't long seated when an old man sat down beside me. I thought, on first seeing him, that his clothes were unusual – black trousers like one would see on a priest or minister, the legs turned up like the old-timers used to do. The material seemed to be calico or heavy flannel; a dark brown collarless coat; a sleeved waistcoat inside that; a gold chain fastened by a clip in the top buttonhole and stretching across his chest into the waistcoat pocket; but most remarkable of all was the small, black woolen hat on top of his head. Indeed, in today's world there would be no such high fashion. The hippies put an end to that in the '60s.

The old fellow took out a pipe, put it in his mouth and lit it without a word or salutation. That didn't upset me as many things could be on a man's mind that would put him in no humour for talking. I glanced at him to see if there was any stir out of any part of his body, but he sat there staring in the direction of a super-market at the top of the street. I couldn't hide my curiosity any longer.

'Is this the town where you were born?' I asked in order to break the silence.

He looked at me as if I had two heads.

'I was born in London,' he replied. 'I was twenty-four years old when I set sail towards this godforsaken town.'

I didn't want to question him too deeply, but, that said, this was an Englishman sitting beside me looking down his nose at a town in my country.

'Listen, my good man,' I said, 'if you feel that life in this coun-try is oppressing you why don't you go back to England?'

'Oh yes,' he said, 'but it isn't so easy for me to do that now.'

The blood was boiling in every inch of my body by now.

'I don't see any fetter or chain tied to you,' I retorted, 'or is it a large holding of land that your people got from the King that keeps you here?'

The old man shifted restlessly in his seat and then he fixed me with his two tiny eyes.

'It's no land, money or gold that fetters me but a strong, tight grip that neither you nor many of your age would understand,' he replied. 'Don't question me any further as you will receive no reply. You're a stranger to this town?' he enquired.

'I suppose you could say that,' I told him. 'My name is Maidhc Dainín Ó Sé. I have a fortnight's work here before I move to some other town. I came up from Kerry today and I hope to meet the local people as long as I am working here.'

This little bit of conversation banished the antipathy that was between us at first.

'I hear that the Irish language has made great progress here lately,' I ventured.

The old boy waited a few seconds before he said a word. Then he took the pipe out of his mouth and put it in his coat pocket.

'To tell you the truth, I belong to another culture that doesn't understand the Irish attitude to their language. The reason I'm here should have been over and done with long ago,' he told me.

I took him at his word. People have many things besides language to bother them.

'You didn't give me your name,' I said inquisitively.

'I didn't,' was all he said.

I stared at him waiting for an answer. He raised his head.

'James Battersby is my name,' he informed me. 'I was born and reared in London. I was educated at Oxford University. It was there I qualified as a lawyer and I was appointed to a high post later on. Without a doubt, many a day and night has passed since . . .'

He moved towards me in his eagerness to talk and he was

getting more interesting with every sentence.

'I suppose,' I said, 'you came across many interesting cases during your lifetime particularly in such a big city as London . . .'

'But didn't I tell you that it was in this country I did most of my work,' he said. 'And I can tell you that I was more than busy here.'

While he was telling me this, his eyes didn't move from the supermarket and restaurant at the top of the street.

'Is there something special about that building up there?' I asked. 'Or are you expecting somebody to come to you from it?'

Old James cleared his throat.

'It wasn't always a supermarket and restaurant,' he informed me. 'It was there the county gaol was and it was there that Lucinda Sly and John Dempsey were hanged. They stood before judge and jury in Deighton Hall, close by. There was a large space in front of the hall and on the day of the hanging the place was thronged with a mob shouting and hurling insults at the two who were to be hanged. It happened on the 30th of March, 1835.'

When I heard that, nothing would satisfy me but to hear every last bit of the story of Lucinda Sly and John Dempsey.

'I see that you're interested in the story,' old James smiled.

I jumped to my feet with excitement.

'You could say that I am,' I exploded. 'This place was under British control. There's no doubt that I'd love to hear the whole story from beginning to end.'

'Yes,' he said with a swagger, 'if you listen to an old man I have plenty of time to relate the tale to you and I can assure you that I am the only person in Carlow that has the right story.'

'I'll come here every evening for the whole fortnight if necessary to hear the whole story from you,' I replied.

'You must be a writer,' he ventured.

'Of sorts,' I said.

'I'll give you the full story,' he promised me, 'on one condition: that you will write it down word for word as I tell it to you and that you put an appendix of your own to it.'

'I promise you sincerely that that's how it will be done,' I told him.

James set his woollen hat on the back of his head and he told me the story of Lucinda Sly, the last woman to be hanged in Carlow, and John Dempsey who was hanged beside her.

# Chapter One

The tragic tale of Lucinda Sly began on a small farm near the town of Tullow in County Carlow. Her family were of English extraction and she had a strong Protestant background. Lucinda Hughes was her maiden name and she was twenty-seven years old when a match was made for her with a small farmer of similar background. His name was Thomas Singleton. When they were two years married, God gave them a son but shortly afterwards the husband became ill. He spent three months in bed at home and eventually died of consumption.

Lucinda was left on her own with a one-year-old child on a small farm with the grass of two cows making it difficult for her to eke out a living. The landlord made no exception for her even though she was a widow. Every three months she would have to pay him his rent just like all the other tenants. She had to harrow and sow in spring and harvest in the autumn like every farmer around her and her neighbours were of little help to her as most of them were up to their necks in hock to the landlord like herself.

Even though Lucinda was not a big woman, she was a powerful

worker. She would be up at the crack of dawn from the first day of spring to the last day of autumn. She knew exactly when to dig the land in order to sow the oats. This she did with a hoe even though the spade and plough were becoming more common about that time. But a small farmer couldn't afford such comfort in those years.

When she made ridges for the planting of the potatoes, the land would be drying out and the weather suitable. 'It's better for the potato seed to be in the house than swimming in the earth' as the proverb has it. When certain farmers would churn milk only once a week in the milking season, Lucinda would churn twice. And, signs on, her butter was famous in Carlow town and its environs. If she were working in the garden or milking the cows in the yard she had no choice but to leave her baby in the house. She had a reasonably easy life as far as the child was concerned, until young Thomas began to crawl and shortly afterwards to strew knick-knacks around the floor. She used the wicker basket in which she brought the turf home as a cradle inside and outside the house. But when the young fellow began to walk she had to think of a different plan.

One day Lucinda was churning. When she had poured the cream into the churn and spilled some on account of Thomas's high jinks, she charged out the door with the child under her oxter. She didn't stop until she reached the horse's stable; she took the halter from a crook on the wall and brought it into the kitchen. She strapped the child in the halter, ripped the reins from one side of it and tied it to the leg of the kitchen table.

'Off you go now and pull the table all over the house,' she said as she went to the bottom of the kitchen again to resume her churning. She had a plan to remedy even the most difficult situation.

The neighbours wondered how Lucinda could make a living out of the small farm that fell to her after her husband's death, especially as she had to pay high rent to a landlord who wouldn't hesitate to evict a tenant if she were even a ha'penny short. But this wonderful, gentle, honest woman did so without complaint and without forcing herself upon her neighbours. No matter what hardship she was forced to endure, her son never slept on an empty stomach.

People say a son should take good care of his mother when he grows to be a man. That's what any Christian would do if he had any conscience at all, after all she had done for him as he was growing. But wait, gentle reader, and your ears will hear a tale they won't believe.

Somehow, this poor woman managed to give him the rudiments of education until he was a strapping young man of eighteen years. This she did but she herself often had to go without.

Even though young Thomas was hard and strong, he gave little by way of help to his mother. On the days she sold her butter, eggs and baked bread on the side of the street in Carlow, off he would go roving the town without any thought about helping her. But he would return when she had sold all her wares accusing her of leaving him hungry throughout the day.

Lucinda wasn't a hard-hearted woman, but having spent many years slaving, sowing and harrowing the land in order to avoid begging, it was time, she thought, for a change.

In olden times, Thursday was always the day for selling butter in Carlow town and one market morning Lucinda told Thomas to fetch the horse from the field and put him under the cart.

'You know what day it is today? . . . Butter market day,' she reminded him.

But Thomas remained at the table guzzling his mother's brown bread and potatoes. Because it was getting late in the morning she told him once again to get up off his lazy backside and harness the horse for the road. But he only squeezed further into the table and stuffed another potato into his mouth.

Lucinda was famous for her butter and her light, tasty brown bread, and now the poor woman was putting the butter into a wicker basket and ten loaves of bread with it. She was easily able to sell them on the side of the street and in this way she had the shop-keepers' profit for herself. The shopkeepers of the town were none too pleased with this as the best of the butter and home-baked bread were going directly to the customer without a penny going to them.

Young Thomas was still sitting at the table when Lucinda was ready for the road. She pushed the basket to the door and pressed it against the frame so that one could go in and out past it. Then she rushed to the bottom of the kitchen, her face red with rage. She took hold of the sweeping brush. She advanced on her son who was just about to drink a mouthful of milk from the bowl he held in his hands. She hit him on the side of the head with the brush. The bowl fell from his hands and he crashed from the chair to the floor. She hit him again on the floor. But, as she did, he caught the head of the brush and pulled it out of her hands. He jumped up. He thrashed poor Lucinda left and right. Then he broke the brush across his knee.

'I'm going to get my clothes and neither you nor any other Christian will see me inside this door again,' he erupted and stormed into his room with a coarse bag he found at the bottom of the kitchen.

Lucinda picked herself up from the ground, her head spinning, not knowing if it was day or night. When she came to herself, she went out, took hold of the horse and guided him in the direction of the big town. If she didn't she wouldn't be able to pay her rent later that month.

Young Thomas Singleton left home that day without much thanks to his mother who had worked tirelessly for years in order to give him a good upbringing. But eaten bread is soon forgotten. Without a doubt, the way he left home broke Lucinda's heart particularly as he had so solemn and quiet a father.

She heard that Thomas was working for a butcher in the town but, because of the abuse he inflicted on her, she wasn't inclined to seek him out or to invite him back home. He was eighteen years old going on nineteen and she considered it was time for him to make his own way in the world.

Life got worse in Ireland at the beginning of the nineteenth century. The landlords were exacting extra rent from their tenants and paying no heed to the Land League who were advancing the case of the small farmers. Life was so hard for Lucinda that she had to sell an in-calf heifer she had intended to keep instead of an old cow (who later fell into a hole on the mountainside and was killed during the winter of 1825).

While she was selling her wares on the side of the street, Lucinda heard from one of her neighbours that a young constable named Thomas Singleton was newly stationed in Bilboa barracks and she questioned her as to whether he was her son. But Lucinda had had no contact with him since the day he walked out the front door. She knew only that he had quit his job in the butcher's shop and that he had left Carlow town a few years previously. The following week while she was selling her butter on the side of the street, she inquired from a constable, who she knew to see, where this new policeman, Thomas Singleton who had come to Bilboa barracks, was from.

'He's a man from these parts,' was the constable's reply without adding or subtracting from the matter.

Lucinda knew from this that the new constable was her son as they were the only Singleton family within forty miles of the town.

# Chapter Two

As time went by and with Lucinda getting older, the farm work and housework were becoming more difficult for her, a middle-aged woman widowed since she was twenty-nine. Without love or a man's arms around her since her husband died, there was a void in her life from that time onwards, a void that only a widow would understand. A widower could go to the pub and drink his fill banishing loneliness, heartbreak and the troubles of life with whiskey or brandy. It would even be possible for him to find a new spouse. But Lucinda had a young child to rear and, in those times, if the neighbours saw a woman drinking in a pub she would be condemned from the altar by the priest or minister.

But now, she had reared her son and he was making his way in the world. She was finding life hard on the farm, every day she was getting older and she was unhappy with her life as it was and as it would be. She swore that she wouldn't be much older before she sought a partner who would come home to her from the fields every evening, who would lie beside her every night, with whom she could discuss the changes and troubles of life as it was all around them. But she was now fifty-two years old and she didn't have the energy she used to have or the radiance in her features that she had twenty years previously. That said, she was an attractive woman for her age. It was always said that every old shoe meets an old stocking.

'My best years have passed me by with my head bent in slavery,' she complained, 'and look at me now – poor, destitute, crushed. The son I reared in poor times when I often went without doesn't bother to come looking for me or to put a shilling in my pocket. No, he spends his time sucking up to bigwigs who would cut the legs off you with a scythe at the turn of a penny.'

She sat by the fire that night with the cat stretched across the ashes in front of her. She looked at the cat.

'I don't know about you,' she said, 'but Lucinda Singleton won't be much longer on her own staring into the fire with nothing but the cold night waiting for her under the blanket.'

The following Thursday when she had caught the horse and put him under the cart, she packed her butter in the basket and the loaves of bread with it as usual. Then she went down to the bedroom. She planned to wear her Sunday best and she took down from the hook a new shawl she had bought at the market before this. She combed and fixed her hair.

Off she went in the direction of the kitchen, humming the air of a song she heard her mother singing when she was about ten years old:

*My young love said to me my mother won't mind*
*And my father won't slight you for your lack of kind*

And she carried on humming until she had the basket in the cart. She untied the reins from a crook on the pier of the gate and jumped into the front of the cart. She took a blackthorn stick that she kept in the cart in case some stranger would attack her when she returned in the dark of night. She hit the horse across the flank to speed him on the road.

When she arrived in town she thought that it was busier than usual.

'Ah yes!' she remembered. 'This is the day of the big fair for in-calf heifers. It falls on the same date every year and it just happens that it falls on a Thursday this year.'

It took her a good while to find a convenient place on the side of the street as there were cattle in the patch where she usually traded. If Lucinda had realised that it was the day of the big fair, she would have set out earlier that morning.

Eventually she found a trading place. It wasn't in the centre of the town but she would have to make do with it. Lucinda usually sold her butter and bread early every Thursday but, because of the two markets, it was late in the evening before she sold the last loaf. The men at the fair were more interested in buying and selling cattle than in buying bread.

There were four young heifers that weren't yet in calf gathered by a farmer on the pavement near Lucinda's horse and cart. Lucinda had neither rest nor peace that day. When the cattle weren't shitting and pissing on the street, they were bellowing and looking in the direction of Lucinda's horse so that few customers came near her stall. The owner of the cattle came out of the pub every twenty minutes or so to see if any buyer was sizing up his beasts and as the day progressed he was getting more scattered with the dint of drink.

It was late in the evening when Lucinda was squeezing the bellyband on the horse. The poor animal was restless having spent the entire day standing under the cart on the side of the street.

'Did you see any buyer looking at my cattle?' the owner asked her. He was barely able to stand after the day's carousing.

'There were five or six buyers around during the day and if you were here instead of having your belly to the counter in Langstrom's tavern, you would have your cattle sold and your money would be in your pocket by now,' Lucinda told him with disdain.

'Ah! My good woman,' he replied, 'there's no need for you to be so sour in the tail of the evening.'

Lucinda tied the basket in the middle of the cart and spoke impatiently:

'I had to stand near your cattle from morning avoiding their dung not to mention their piss running under my feet,' she retorted.

Drunk and awkwardly the farmer begged her pardon.

'My name is Walter Sly,' he informed her. 'It's hard for me to be right without a wife at home to bake a cake of bread for me or to patch a hole in my trousers, not to mention to keep me company by the fire.'

Though she gave no sign, Lucinda's heart softened when she heard that, especially since she was in the same predicament herself.

'It's time for me to be heading for home,' she said, yanking the horse's reins to guide him out to the middle of the street.

'A thousand pardons for the way the cattle behaved. Two of them were bulling. That is why they were so restless when I left them standing. I didn't get your name,' the farmer replied drunkenly.

'Lucinda Singleton,' she informed him. 'Go on,' she urged the horse on the road.

'Isn't it lovely for you to be going home to your husband and family,' Sly ventured.

'The side of my hearth is as empty as your own,' she told him.

'Lucinda Singleton? . . . Is there any chance you would be related to Thomas Singleton, the policeman in Bilboa barracks?' he wondered.

Lucinda didn't tell him how her son left her without a word of thanks for all she had done for him in his early years and she hadn't forgotten the beating he gave her before he left.

'Maybe there would, but it would be far out,' she replied as she took to the road.

Walter Sly was just about to go back into the pub when a buyer he knew from Ballinasloe came the way. Although they were never over overly friendly, the buyer badly wanted the cattle and Sly wanted rid of them before another hard winter hit him with his farm bared to the earth because he had too much stock. As soon as he examined Sly's cattle, the buyer couldn't find fault with them because they were well-fed, big-boned and bred for meat.

'Put a price on them,' said Power, the buyer.

By this time, Walter Sly realised that Power badly wanted his cattle.

'Seven pounds apiece,' Sly demanded.

Power stepped backwards.

'The drink has gone to your head,' he replied. 'I'll give you five pounds ten shillings apiece for them and if you aren't satisfied with that we'll split up immediately.'

Walter Sly knew that he had got a good offer for the cattle. He spat on the palm of his right hand and stretched it out to Power.

'It's a bargain,' he said.

They both headed for Langstrom's where Sly would get his money and they would drink to the bargain.

On his way home that night, Walter Sly couldn't put the woman he had wrangled with only that evening on the side of the street out of his mind. Instead of guiding his horse home to Oldleighlin, it occurred to him that it would be a good plan to go to Bilboa barracks to have a chat with Constable Thomas Singleton. What that woman said to him was still irritating him.

This wasn't Walter Sly's first time looking for a wife. But he had failed miserably every time because of his drinking and the bad reputation he had among women. But he was determined to straighten himself out, that is if he were able to entice Lucinda Singleton into his household before too long.

Walter was a few years with the half century and he felt that Lucinda was about the same age. He badly wanted a woman around the house to milk the cows with him morning and evening, who would do the churning once a week during the milking season and who would do the baking. He considered himself to be reasonably good-looking even though his eyes were clouded by drink when he had spoken with her. Most of the women he knew during his life were unscrupulous women who would drink with him in the back room of the pub until they had spent his every last penny and not one of them had ever milked a cow. Some of them, perhaps, were already married but had no regard for man or for sacrament. Often Sly would have to fight the husband when he was found with the wife. Fighting and misfortune were Walter Sly's lot since he came to the age of reason, that is, if he ever attained it.

He almost fell from his horse when he stuck his boot in the stirrup outside Bilboa barracks. He tied the reins to the pier of the garden gate and took a bottle of whiskey from a pocket in the saddle. He staggered up the pavement and knocked drunkenly on the door.

The door opened and there stood Constable Thomas Singleton.

'Is it yourself, Walter?' he greeted him. 'What's up with you so late in the night? Don't tell me you had a row with horse traders again or is some woman's husband after you?'

'Oh, no!' spluttered Sly. 'But something entirely different.'

When the constable saw the bottle of whiskey, and bearing in mind the desire for the drop they both had, he opened the door.

'Come in, come in,' he said. 'It's a while since we had a drink together. It's not the smell of the wind I'm getting from your breath, whatever tavern you left.'

Singleton took the bottle of whiskey from Sly and led him into the office. Then he went into the kitchen and came back with two glasses.

Sly sat on a sugawn chair at the side of the table pondering how he would convey what was in his mind to his friend, particularly as there was a chance that Singleton might be related to the woman at the fair.

'I'm coming straight from the market in Carlow town,' Sly informed the constable.

Singleton looked at him keenly with a smile on his face.

'I'd believe that,' he laughed. 'Were you buying or selling?'

Walter Sly stirred in his chair.

'Oh, selling,' he informed him, 'and I'm very glad to have gotten rid of my cattle before I'd have to graze them on the side of the road again this winter. I had to do it last winter and I hadn't a day's peace until the land dried in the spring and the grass began to grow.'

'I remember,' Singleton assured him. 'Your neighbours had a path worn to the barracks telling me to take you to court and to confiscate your cattle and horses. But I was always able to come around them.'

'Oh, Thomas, isn't that why I brought you the bottle of whiskey. I'm very grateful for what you did for me,' Sly lied.

Singleton poured a generous measure into each glass. They spent the next half hour discussing the ups and downs of the world while all the time Sly was awaiting an opportunity to question him about the woman he met at the market. Eventually he got his chance.

'I can't understand, Walter,' the constable said, 'why a strong, healthy man like you with a nice farm of land within four miles of the town never took a wife.'

Sly moved uncomfortably in his chair and cleared his throat.

'Twice,' he told him, 'the match was made with two different women. I don't know what happened to the first woman but she went away two nights before the knot was to be tied. I got a note that was pushed under my door in the dark of night telling me that she was breaking the match. I think one of my neighbours must have told her that I was fond of the drink. When the second woman sent her intermediary to discuss the terms of the match and I told him I was a Protestant, he took off down the road and I haven't had trace nor tidings of him since.'

Singleton poured more whiskey in Sly's glass and remarked:

'You were unfortunate in life without a doubt. Those Catholics, you know, were always as obstinate as a tinker's mule when it comes to the question of religion. But, Walter, it might be no harm if you eased off on the drink. I've noticed lately that even the slightest irritation makes you impatient.'

Sly waited a few seconds before he answered him; then he straightened himself in his chair.

'You're entirely right, Thomas,' he agreed. 'But if I had a wife at home who would cook my meals and work hand-in-hand with me, I'd not be in the pub but sitting by the fire at night laying out the farm work for the coming season. Oh boy! Wouldn't I be comfortable and happy in my chair with the love of my life across the hearth darning the sole of a stocking or putting a patch in my trousers. Talking of fine women, I met one today at the market, a handsome woman about my own age.'

When Singleton heard this, he tried to make light of the matter.

'For God's sake, Walter,' he advised him, 'stay away from the women you meet in the back rooms of pubs. They'll rob you or else one of their husbands will kill you.'

Sly jumped to his feet.

'But Thomas,' he began, 'you don't understand at all. This woman I'm talking about, I didn't meet her in any back room but on the side of the street selling her bread and butter. I can tell you, Thomas, though she is moving on in years she was energetic and spirited. To tell you the truth she gave out to me for leaving my cattle and for being drunk, and she was entirely right.'

Singleton looked sharply at Sly.

'Well,' he said, 'if she's that handsome I suppose she has a fine strong man at home minding the farm.'

'No,' Sly informed him. 'In the short conversation we had, it slipped from her that she was a widow. And wait until you hear her name . . . it's your own, Singleton'.

The policeman sat back staring Walter directly in the eye.

'By any chance,' he said, 'did she call herself Lucinda Singleton?'

'Look, now that you mention Lucinda,' Walter replied, 'that's the name she gave herself.'

Singleton thought for a minute. He had had no contact with his mother since that fateful day he left her house and he hadn't been next or near her since then. Then, suddenly, she crops up in the conversation between himself and Walter Sly. He had intended many times to go home and beg forgiveness for the beating he gave her. But his courage failed every time.

'Had she a horse and cart with her butter and bread in a wicker basket?' he asked, tears welling up in his eyes.

'She had a horse and cart with a basket sure enough,' Walter replied, 'but she had sold everything by the time we had our conversation.'

Sly looked straight at Singleton.

'She is your mother, isn't she?' he demanded.

'She is,' the policeman admitted, 'though it's likely she would deny that she is any relation of mine.'

'Oh for God's sake! And I was thinking on my way here from Carlow that if you were any way related to her you would put in a good word for me,' Sly ventured.

Singleton laughed when he heard that.

'Oh, you scoundrel,' he rounded on him. 'That's what brought you here and it wasn't for friendship or the good of my health. To tell you the truth, if I put in a word for you, it would have the opposite effect . . . but I'll tell you how to get to her and if she is willing to go to the well, so to speak, the second time you should listen carefully to me. She never liked to see a man drunk. Now, if you want to attract her, she sells her bread and butter in Carlow every Thursday during the milking season. My advice to you is to keep off the drink on the day you meet her and dress yourself in your Sunday clothes. When she has everything sold and the work of the day is behind her invite her to have a meal with you.'

Walter Sly's eyes were jumping in his head with excitement.

'I'll do better than that,' he offered. 'I'll buy a couple of loaves of bread from her. Oh, Thomas, I'm more than grateful to you and I promise you that if things work out between me and your mother that I won't forget you when the time comes. I have neither chick nor child and I have a fine farm of land.'

They finished the bottle of whiskey before Sly faced for home.

# Chapter Three

The morning after the fair, it was the cattle bellowing out in the field that woke Walter Sly, his head hanging from the side of the bed, his mouth as dry as a coarse bag, his head throbbing. He sat up in the bed and slowly and carefully put a foot out on the cold clay floor. He pulled up his trousers and walked unsteadily towards the kitchen. Bran, his dog, was sitting on the floor; he hadn't had a bite of food from his master since the previous morning.

Sly headed for the dresser at the bottom of the kitchen, took the jug of sour milk and raised it to his head. He drank the contents of the jug, lifted his left leg and broke wind.

'Ah, boy,' he exclaimed, 'I feel better now.'

It was then he remembered that he hadn't milked the cows when he returned the previous night. He poured water from a bucket that was on a stool at the bottom of the kitchen into a dish on the table, plunged his hands into the dish and splashed the water on his face. A person couldn't find a better way to wake himself up.

'I'd better milk the cows before breakfast,' he said, 'before their udders burst.'

By the time he had eight cows milked and the milk strained into the dishes in the dairy he was sweating profusely.

'Oh! The scourge of drink,' he lamented.

When he had the cream skimmed from the previous morning's milk, mess from the buttermilk made in the three-legged pot hanging on the crane over the fire, the potatoes heating in the hot ashes ready for breakfast and four hens' eggs boiled in a saucepan on the embers at the side of the fire, Sly was starving. Bran would have to wait until his master had his belly full.

When he had eaten his fill, he put the two potatoes that were left over as well as a splash of fresh milk and a hunk of meat in Bran's bowl; he made mess for the hens and threw it out to them at the bottom of the haggard. His cows had knocked a strip off the boundary ditch between his land and Ben Stacey's, his neighbour. There was an ongoing dispute about this over the years. Sly had the same trouble with John Griffin, another neighbour. What seldom happens is wonderful and he saw no trace of his neighbours that day, something for which he was extremely grateful. His head was splitting from the previous day's drinking and he would need all his wits to come around Lucinda Sly without spoiling things.

'Maybe this is my last chance to get a wife,' Sly considered, 'I don't want to grow old on my own.'

He planned to have a couple of glasses of whiskey and a couple of bottles of porter every night until Monday and then he wouldn't taste a drop again until Friday. He expected he would have made contact with Lucinda Singleton by then and that he would have a good idea as to what his chances were.

Sly was succeeding with his plan about drinking. Though his friends in the tavern didn't understand why he was easing off on the drink, he was too smart to inform them that a woman was the reason for this. He even kept away from those in the company who would spur him to drinking. He would leave the tavern as early as eight o'clock. One of his companions opined that the age was catching him and that his stomach wasn't healthy enough to deal with large amounts of drink.

During the following week he was determined to make his own butter on the Wednesday and bring it on the Thursday to the shop in Carlow where he sold it. That way, he would be in Carlow on the same day that Lucinda Sly sold her wares on the side of the street. He contacted the shopkeeper he dealt with and he was happy to stock his butter every Thursday.

The following Thursday dawned without a cloud in the sky. Sly hadn't had a drink since the previous Monday night. He hadn't felt as healthy in many a day but his stomach was rumbling with excitement. He put a couple of potatoes to roast in the hot ashes while he was milking the cows.

When he had done the household chores and had eaten breakfast, it was time to ready himself for the day and the task before him. He took the boiling kettle from the crane over the fire and poured some water from it into a dish on the table, got his razor and stropped twenty times on a strap of leather that was hanging on the side of the window. He wanted a clean shave without cutting himself under his ear or nose and with no patches on his face as was usual. This was a special day. His clothes from his shoes up to the few ribs of hair on his head would have to blend with his clean-shaven face and everything would have to be exact. Because he had no polish to shine his shoes he got an old rag and rubbed it in the soot that was baked onto the back of the fireplace and applied it to them. Before he left the house to go to Carlow he hurried down the room to where an old mirror was hanging. Then he put the small, black woollen hat he wore on Sunday on his head and regarded himself in the mirror. 'By God! Walter,' he beamed. 'Even if you are middle-aged, you will get the women to look at you yet.'

The clock was striking midday before the horse had eaten a handful of oats and was saddled for the road. Sly put an extra half-stone of oats in a small bag that he would hang on the hook of the saddle if he were going on a long journey. Who knows? Maybe this would be a long day. He hung another little bag containing the butter from the week's churning on the other side of the saddle.

As soon as Sly reached town he stabled his horse in the shopkeeper's stable and gave him his bag of butter. The shopkeeper weighed the butter on his scales. Sly suspected that the shopkeeper, John Cooney, didn't let the scales settle properly.

'One stone and three pounds of butter,' the shopkeeper informed him. 'That's seventeen pounds at threepence-farthing a pound.'

'Hold it a minute, John,' Sly interrupted. 'Did you ever hear from the priest you go to Mass to about the sin of the weighing?'

'I must admit,' John replied innocently, 'that I didn't. I don't think it's written in any catechism of the Catholic Church.'

'It should be,' Sly said mockingly. 'I heard in a sermon from the minister in the church that I go to, that the sin of the weighing is the most common sin on shopkeepers' souls when they go before God.'

'Tell me about the sin of the weighing,' the shopkeeper replied, 'because the priest in the church were I go said that the worst sin is for a man to chase a family from their holding and then to grab it for himself.'

It was said that Walter Sly had chased a family from their holding which was bounding his because he was given a claim to it by the Crown as he was a Protestant.

'Put the butter back on the scales,' Sly ordered him, ignoring the hint the shopkeeper threw in his direction.

This Cooney did, placing weights measuring seventeen pounds on the other side of the scales. The butter raised the seventeen pounds in weights.

'Put another pound weight on the scales,' Sly said triumphantly, 'and that will level the scales.'

The shopkeeper did as he was told. Then the weights went down slowly.

'What did I tell you?' said the shopkeeper. 'There are too many weights on the scales now.'

'Try the half pound weight,' Sly demanded with rancour in his voice.

'I will not,' Cooney countered. 'Your horse will have eaten its value in hay before you take him from my stable this evening.'

The shopkeeper made up the price of the butter and extended it to Sly.

'I have more important things to be doing than listening to the prattling of a gombeen on the side of the street,' was all Sly said.

He turned on his heel and dashed out the door leaving the shopkeeper with a satisfied grin on his face.

The main street was crammed from top to bottom with stalls full of goods expertly laid out by housewives with a view to attracting the eye of prospective buyers: some of them selling their butter, others selling potatoes, cabbage and vegetables; three or four more standing by the rails of their horse carts with every screech coming from the bonhams inside the rails.

'Nora, where is Jack?' Sly inquired of a woman who was standing by a rail of bonhams.

'He is in the place you usually are,' she replied sourly, 'throwing back the drink.'

Sly cast his eye on the litter of bonhams.

'They are at least three months old,' he observed judging their age.

'Put another fortnight with it,' Nora answered. 'I'd prefer to be rid of them. We have only two pits of potatoes left and two sows to feed for the winter . . . My soul to the devil, Walter, you're all dressed up today. If I didn't know you as well as I do, I'd say you were on the lookout for a wife. But I think you're past it. Ha! Ha!'

When he heard that, he turned his back on Nora and faced up the street on his mission.

He wasn't long walking when he saw Lucinda Singleton in a convenient patch across the street. This is the woman who had distracted his senses all week. His eyes were wide open this time as he hadn't put a drink to his lips for four days. Sly walked slowly towards Lucinda pretending to examine the loaves of bread and the bowl of butter in front of her. She looked carefully at this well-dressed man who was standing before her.

'I'll take two loaves of bread,' Sly said steadily. 'I heard that you sell the best bread in town.'

'Don't mind your soft talk because you won't get it a penny cheaper. Three pence ha'penny to you and to everyone else,' Lucinda replied.

She wrapped paper around the two loaves and gave them to him.

'Three pence ha'penny apiece – that's seven pence,' she said curtly.

'And they're worth a lot more,' Sly replied gently. Lucinda stared at him.

'Do I know you, or have I seen you before?' she demanded.

Sly smiled.

'Do you remember last Thursday, the in-calf heifer sale?'

Lucinda's eyes jumped in her head when she heard this.

'You,' was all she could say. 'The rogue with the cattle! I can tell you that you had enough to drink that evening.'

'To tell you the truth, Lucinda . . . that's your name, isn't it? I had enough, all right. I came to town today especially to apologise to you for my conduct last Thursday,' Sly replied.

Lucinda laughed.

'You did indeed,' she said. 'Off with you now and don't be mocking an old widow.'

Sly moved a step closer to her.

'I'm seldom like that,' he lied, 'and if I can do you a favour to make up for it, I will.'

Sly's words moved her.

'Forget about it. I forgive you,' she said softly.

When Sly saw her being moved, he thought that this was his chance.

'Do you know,' he ventured, 'as reparation for my sins, maybe I could buy you a bite to eat later on.'

When she heard this, Lucinda looked at him doubtfully.

'I hardly know you,' she retorted. 'How do I know that you're not a murderer or one of those scamps that's forever luring gullible women on the road?'

Sly laughed heartily on hearing this.

'I am Walter Sly,' he told her, 'fifty-two years old and never had the courage to seek a wife . . . I live on the finest farm in Oldleighlin. Question any of my neighbours about my pedigree and I promise you that they won't have a thing to say against me except that I drink the odd drink. Yes! And I wouldn't do that but for the fact that there's nothing before me at home only the cold walls of the house and a dog in the corner. If I had a wife at home, I would be in a hurry to return to her.'

Lucinda stood listening, at the same time sizing him up as he stood in front of her. After a while she spoke:

'I can't leave my bread and butter on the side of the street to go rambling with you. Come this way in two hours and if I have sold my wares, then maybe I'll let you buy me some food.'

'You know,' Sly replied excitedly, 'I have some things to do around town myself; I'll be back to you in a while.'

Sly went down the street like a swallow in flight humming to himself.

'A good start is half the work,' he observed. 'Oh boy, I'd better take it easy with her and not show too much enthusiasm. What was the advice her son Thomas gave me? Yes, that she was a shrewd woman.'

Meanwhile Lucinda paid extra attention to her stall, at the same time thinking deeply.

'Maybe I saw the worst side of him on market day,' she considered. 'Without a doubt a man has a right to drink a drop now and again as long as he doesn't make a tramp out of himself. When I see him clean-shaven today, upon my soul but he is a fine man. I suppose it will do no harm to get to know him better. I have spent most of my life on my own and I'm tired of it. Maybe my chance has come today.'

Lucinda had sold her bread and butter within an hour and a half, the basket was tied in the cart and a small sack of corn was hanging at the horse's head. She looked up and down the street. She was thinking that it was time the man who was to take her to the eating house appeared.

She hadn't long to wait as Sly was coming up the street in a great hurry.

'Now, my good woman,' he panted, 'have you your mind made up or will I be shortening the road for home?'

'It's not every day a woman gets invited to a meal,' Lucinda smiled.

The two of them walked up the street together in the direction of the eating house and all eyes were on them.

# Chapter Four

After Walter Sly and Lucinda Singleton had eaten their meal on the Thursday and had come to know each other better, even though Sly had a strong desire for drink, he didn't mention a hotel or tavern while he was in her company. Lucinda was impressed by his demeanour that evening but it was a little early, with a long road ahead of them, to make any judgement. Sly questioned her about the place she came from.

'It's called Tullow,' she informed him, 'a country town like any small town in Ireland.'

Sly knew the county well, not to mention the lie of the land. Anybody who was involved in buying and selling horses would be travelling east, west, up and down through the countryside.

Before they parted that evening, Sly told her that he would be travelling closeby Tullow the following Sunday. He told her that a farmer who lived near there was looking for a working horse and that he, Sly, had one. Without a doubt, there wasn't a word of the truth in his statement. He wanted to cast his eye over her holding to assess it as a dowry, that is if things developed that far. He was greedy for land since he was a young man.

'Why don't you come to my house on Sunday?' Lucinda suggested. 'I'll have some food ready for you.'

'I'll be there about two o'clock,' Sly replied, barely concealing his excitement.

Sly walked Lucinda to her horse, which she had tied to a ring at the side of the street; he put the horse under the cart and made sure that the horse's harness was properly fitted for the road. No sooner had Lucinda and her horse passed the top of the street than Sly headed for Langstrom's tavern and his old ways. He would have until Sunday to recover.

When Lucinda reached home that Thursday evening, her two cows hadn't yet been milked. Having unharnessed the horse and put him grazing in the haggard, she milked her cows, strained the milk and poured it into the dishes in the dairy. It was many a long day since she had been so satisfied in her mind.

'Now,' she sighed, 'maybe after all my years of slavery God will grant me ease for the rest of my life. Oh, when I think of the hungry years I spent digging and harrowing, sowing and harvesting to pay my rent, not to mention having to put a bite in my son's mouth and in my own ... Yes, and to put clothes on our bones, he had little thanks but to half kill me before he headed out into the world. But, that said, if he came in the door this minute, I'd forgive him everything ... Ah yes, Walter Sly ... Is he as well-to-do as I sensed from his talk? A woman of my age should be careful. The next day I go to Carlow, I'll enquire as to his pedigree. Who would know him better than the shopkeeper he sells his butter to? I am at an age now where there is no room for making a mistake. It's a fine thing to marry into a farm as long as I wouldn't be a slave. I have done my slaving.'

It was late in the night when Sly arrived home. He was barely able to take the saddle off his horse in his drunken stupor. When he had ripped the buckle under the horse's belly, the saddle fell to the ground. He took off the headstall and let the horse off through the barn down to the field.

'Bad cess to you! Isn't there a great hunger on you? By God, there will be no cow milked till morning. I'm tired from the work of the day,' he yawned.

Sly sat in his chair in the corner, took his pipe from the hole in the hob and pushed the chair up on its two back legs, a habit he had when he was thinking deeply. A good day's work, he felt. His chances of securing a wife were good, a wife who was accustomed to farm work, churning, who could sew a patch in the backside of trousers, bake a cake of bread, and split seed potatoes for the spring planting. Wouldn't it be good to come in from the field after a long day's work to a hot meal on the table before him? But he thought it would be some time before that happened. He would have to be careful as this was his last chance to find a wife. No intermediary came to his house with an account of a match these twenty Shrovetides past. When he had thought enough about what was before him, Sly got up from the chair, broke wind and staggered to the bedroom.

Lucinda rose early the following Sunday morning and put a hunk of pork into the pot on the hook over the open fire. She would boil it for an hour and then put it on the hot coals on the side of the fire. That way, the meat and green cabbage would be softly boiling while she attended the service at the Protestant church a mile down the road.

In his own house in Oldleighlin, Walter Sly was up at the break of day in order to have the housework done and himself well shaved for the occasion before him. While he was milking the cows, a thought occurred to him that would make a good man of him in Lucinda's eyes. He would call into Bilboa police station on his way to her house and attempt to entice Thomas Singleton to go with him for a reconciliation with his mother.

The clock on the kitchen wall was striking for midday as Walter Sly lifted the latch on the door to set out on his journey. He took the brush from the kitchen to sweep any dirt or dust that might be on the floor or on the seats of the trap onto the ground. Maybe Lucinda would go for a ride with him towards Kilkenny. That is where many of the gentry travelled in their horses and coaches when they were courting young women. 'Yes, if it is good enough for the gentry, it is good enough for Walter Sly,' he figured.

When he reached the barracks in Bilboa, Sly tied the horse's reins to an iron ring that was embedded in the pillar of the gate for that purpose. He hurried towards the door. He was just about to knock on the door when it opened. There, standing before him, was Constable Thomas Singleton who appeared to be in a great hurry. Behind him was Marie, his wife.

'By God, you're visiting early this blessed day, Walter,' Singleton observed. 'Is it something urgent? We're on our way to the service in the church.'

'It is and it isn't,' Sly replied. 'I'm travelling to your mother's house and I was thinking since I heard about the argument between you, that it is time to hang your weapons on the wall and make up.'

Singleton laughed doubtfully.

'Don't tell me,' he said, 'that the two of you are . . . well, you know . . . friendly with each other. By God! But you're a terrible rogue, Walter. It is many years since I left home and the way I parted with my mother still troubles me. Many times I planned to go home and fix things up but a week went by and a year went by and it is now so long that I would be ashamed to go into the house without a prior arrangement.'

Sly thought for a few seconds.

'I understand your plight well,' he assured him, 'and I say that now is your chance to put things right before it is too late for both of you. By the way, I know that it troubles your mother as much as it troubles you.'

Singleton thought for a minute.

'Do you know, Walter,' he began, 'you could let her know how upset I am for what I did to her and that I would have gone home long ago only that I was ashamed. Maybe if I were to go with you today it might be boiling water I'd get in the heels running down the road . . . If she responds favourably to what you say on my behalf I promise you that I will go home before the end of the week and I will bring Marie to meet her. Now we have to hurry to church. The minister doesn't like people to be late for service!'

Walter Sly faced the road with a satisfied mind. It was a twelve-mile journey from the barracks to Lucinda's house but that was nothing to the horse or to himself. Sly often travelled a hundred miles to a fair. He even went to the Clifden fair in County Galway and that was well over a hundred miles.

Because this Sunday was a fine day, the road he was travelling was fairly busy; coaches were coming against him not to mention horses with riders on their backs, with more coming behind him and hurrying past.

When Sly suspected that he was getting close to the place where Lucinda lived, he stopped in front of a thatched house on the side of the road. The woman of the house was standing at her ease at the threshold watching the coaches and the pedestrians hurrying over and back.

'God bless you, my good woman,' he began, 'would you know where Lucinda Singleton lives?'

When she heard this, the woman looked at him shrewdly. It was a few seconds before she replied.

'A little way down the road in the direction you are travelling. There is a boreen on your right. It is the first house down that road,' she replied, still looking at him inquisitively.

Sly guided the horse down the boreen just as he had been instructed. He saw the house a few hundred yards from him with farm buildings at the back. He pulled on the reins and stopped the horse in the middle of the road. He looked carefully at the fields behind the house. 'I suppose,' he reflected, 'they would be sufficient for a dowry. At my age I have no choice. This is my last chance.' He guided the horse and trap up near the gable of the house. He jumped to the ground from the trap. He was about to unyoke the horse when the thought struck him that Lucinda might like to go for a ride out in the air. In any case, he was not a man who would be at his ease sitting in a stranger's kitchen.

Sly knocked on the frame of the door even though it was open. Lucinda was bent over the pot of potatoes testing them to see if they were boiled.

'Come in! Come in!' she invited him. Sly walked slowly into the kitchen.

'Oh, Lucinda,' he began, 'the water came to my teeth when I got the fine smell of food as I was walking towards the door. Pork and green cabbage I would say.'

Lucinda put the cover on the pot and took a step backwards, her face covered with sweat from being bent over the fire. She turned towards Sly, a glow on her face like that of a young girl meeting the love of her heart for the first time. She stretched out her hand towards him and shook it heartily.

'I hope you are hungry,' she said. 'It will be ten minutes before the potatoes are boiled. Sit down on the settle.'

Sly sat on the settle watching her every move. He was thinking that, even though neither of them was in the bloom of youth, it was good that they wouldn't spend the rest of their lives alone. But, that said, their friendship hadn't grown to that as yet. That was obvious from the signs that were there the last time they met.

Sly observed the woman preparing the meal. He was thinking

what a fine life he would have if he managed to sweep her off her feet. If he were married to this woman, with all her talents, his farm would be one of the finest in County Carlow.

'Sit down to the table, Walter,' she invited him.

Sly couldn't take his eyes off the table as he approached it. One wouldn't see the like of the meal that was on it even in the land-lord's house on Sunday. 'This woman has to be on the lookout for a partner just like I am. God in heaven, wouldn't a glass of whiskey go down well now,' he thought, his body trembling all over.

'Here we are now. I hope you like pork and the cabbage is very good at this time of year,' Lucinda said in order to put him at his ease.

They both sat down and began to eat. They made light conver-sation while they were eating and it was during the meal that Walter mentioned Thomas Singleton. When she heard her son's name, silence fell for a few seconds. Then Lucinda spoke in a firm voice:

'Are you very friendly with my son, Thomas?' she asked of him.

'Upon my soul, I am,' Sly informed her. 'He has done me a cou-ple of favours over the past few years. A gentleman.'

Lucinda shook her head.

'I'm afraid, Walter, that unless a miracle happened since he left the shelter of this house you don't know him rightly,' Lucinda lamented.

Sly washed down a chunk of pork with a mouthful of milk and moved back a half foot from the table.

'Oh, Lucinda,' he looked at her, 'he told me about the bad

feeling that grew up between you. He told me that he was young when it happened and that he had no sense. He often intended to seek you out and ask your forgiveness, but, every time he came within a mile of your house, the shame wouldn't let him stand before you and say that he was sorry for the hardship he caused you.'

Lucinda laid her knife and fork on the table and looked straight at Sly.

'Did he say that?' she asked him softly.

Sly looked at her earnestly.

'As sure as my parents are buried in the graveyard outside Carlow town, he said that to me,' he promised her. 'Do you know that I would like to bring the two of you together and make friends of you again?'

'Do you think if I invited him and his family to come to my house that he would come?' she asked with a glimmer of hope in her voice.

'I am certain that he would,' he told her.

During the meal, they got to know each other much better. Walter let Lucinda know the important work her son was doing for the locality and for the Crown. He let her know that he would personally see to it that Thomas would come to her house without delay.

Even though their conversation was sensible and personal, neither Lucinda nor Walter went overboard. Sly told her how lonely his life was, particularly during the long winter nights when he would be sitting alone in the kitchen, the north or east wind whistling angrily around the chimney outside.

Without a doubt, Lucinda had a couple of questions about what she had heard from people she knew on the streets of Carlow. She felt it was right to question him about his carousing in the taverns. It was best to question him now before things went too far and she was tied to a drunkard.

'Walter,' she said, 'it has come to my attention that you spend a lot of time drinking and carousing in the taverns.'

The mouthful of milk Sly was drinking almost choked him with the start he got at Lucinda's question.

'Who told you that?' he stuttered. 'I'm not denying that I take a couple of drinks but I wouldn't call it carousing. Some of my work involves buying and selling horses along with my work on the farm. It is the custom when an animal is bought or sold to have a few drinks to seal the bargain. Maybe, now and then, I would have a drink or two over and above but I promise you if I had a good wife at home that I wouldn't be drinking in the taverns all night. I'd have a drink or two when the bargain was made and head straight for home to my darling wife.'

Sly spoke so earnestly that Lucinda believed every word.

That Sunday evening Walter Sly swept Lucinda off her feet. They left her house together and went for a drive in Sly's trap. He guided the horse in the direction of Kilkenny. Lucinda hadn't felt so alive since she was a young girl travelling the same road with her husband, Thomas Singleton.

Sly described the advantages she would have living on a big farm and the comforts she would have there. He let her know that he would be willing to put her name on his farm if they were married.

They decided that Sunday that they would meet at least once a week to get to know each other better. It wouldn't always be in Lucinda's house that they would meet because Sly knew that Lucinda wanted to cast her eye on the house and the holding she might marry into. She herself had a small house and holding from which she eked a living and kept the landlord from her door when times were tough. After all that, she didn't want to buy a pig in a poke.

# Chapter Five

Having taken Lucinda home, Walter Sly guided his horse in the direction of Carlow town. It was almost a week since he had had a drink and his desire for it was pricking him constantly but he considered it worth the trouble if he managed to entice Lucinda to marry him even though it bothered him that she was getting long in the tooth and there was no chance that they would have a family. But yes! She would be a good workhorse. It wasn't for racing he wanted her.

He tied the horse's reins to the ring on the side of the pavement directly outside Langstrom's tavern and looked at the door with a light heart. It wasn't open yet. 'It has got to be close to seven o'clock,' Sly thought to himself. He looked around in case there was a policeman strolling around the street. He knocked on the door of the shop next to the tavern. He knew John Cooney, the shopkeeper, very well. Wasn't it in his shop he sold his butter and eggs and wasn't it there he bought flour and any other food he needed?

'Is it yourself, Walter?' Cooney greeted him on opening the

door. 'I haven't seen you any night for a week. I heard that you have given up the drink and that you are looking for a wife. Is there any truth in the rumour?'

'Stop your mocking and take the lock from the gate into your yard until I unyoke my horse and put him out of the people's sight in your stable,' was Sly's reply.

The shopkeeper opened the gate at the side of his house and beckoned to Sly to guide his horse and trap in. When he had put everything in order, Sly thanked the shopkeeper.

'Lock the gate when you are leaving,' Cooney ordered him. 'I'm going to bed early tonight. Tomorrow is another working day.'

Sly headed for the Langstrom's tavern. It was still locked. He knocked vigorously on the door a couple of times. After a short while, the tavern keeper spoke from inside.

'Who's out?' he demanded.

'Open the door, you stallion,' Walter barked. 'It's Walter Sly.'

The owner opened the door with a smirk on his face.

'There are the world of stories about Walter Sly going the streets these days,' he began.

'And what kind of story, or stories, about me are in the old hags' mouths?' Sly demanded sourly.

'That you are spending your time with a great lady . . . a widow with land and wealth along with it; that you are finished with drinking and carousing. Look, Walter,' he said, 'come in, in the name of God, before the police see you.'

Sly strode in angrily. He was able to make fun of other people but couldn't take it himself.

'Into the back room,' Langstrom steered him. 'You know that seven o'clock is closing time.'

Even so, Sly stood stubbornly at the counter.

'Is there anybody in the back room,' he demanded.

'Six,' Langstrom informed him.

'Now,' Sly turned on him, 'tell me where you are getting your information because, as far as I am concerned, it doesn't concern you at all.'

Langstrom understood that Sly was angry as there was fire in every word that came from his mouth.

'Ah! Take it easy, Walter,' he placated him. 'I was only rising you.'

'You know that mocking is catching. Keep your rumours to yourself if you please and to show you that there's no truth in them put a glass of whiskey in front of me,' Sly demanded.

The owner didn't say another word but hurried behind the counter and poured the drink.

Walter Sly walked into the back room when he had paid for his drink. There were five men before him, sitting, as was their custom, around a table playing cards and a middle-aged woman seated on a stool by the wall with a drink in her hand keeping an eye on every card that hit the table.

After Sly had greeted them, and they him, he sat beside the woman. They knew each other well. Frances Campbell was her name and she was married to a bigwig who owned land in three counties not to mention the fact that he was a member of the House of Lords in Westminster. From the first day they married, they never agreed. She married him so that she would have a fine, free life with money to spend as she pleased. She had a reputation for the men and, in those times, you would seldom see a woman in the back room or at the counter of a tavern. It wasn't like that for Frances; she spent her time in the back rooms of taverns and hotels knocking back drink with the gentlemen, if that is the right word for them, and particularly in the company of her own kind who would need to have fat purses.

As soon as the five men had finished their game, they invited Walter and Frances to join them at the table but they declined. Sly said that he would be too busy quenching the week's thirst to be watching five rogues reneging cards at every opportunity that came their way.

Like every woman in Carlow, Frances Campbell knew everybody's business. Sly bought another drink for himself and one for her. Having discussed the state of the country and the way the poor were destroying the locality, Sly stood another drink. Frances didn't refuse it.

After the two of them had downed four or five drinks, Frances moved closer to Sly and spoke softly to him:

'Is it true what I hear, Walter?' she began.

Sly knew what was bothering her but he had no intention of satisfying her curiosity.

'Out with it, Frances, with whatever you want to know . . . that is if it is any of your business,' Sly challenged her.

She stirred uneasily in her chair.

'I always thought you were fond of me,' she replied sadly.

'I'd thank you to keep what happened between us under your hat,' Sly retorted. 'If your husband heard about it he would banish me to New South Wales with the criminals of Ireland.'

She elbowed him in his chest.

'An old widow with a couple of acres of poor land who will turn her backside to you in bed as soon as she gets inside your front door,' she taunted him. 'I heard that she is almost sixty years old. I am not yet fifty. It is said that the well dries up in most women when they hit their mid fifties. Along with that you will have to be at home beside her every night for the rest of your life.'

She ordered a couple of drinks from the owner. That gave Walter time to consider what she had said.

'Look Frances,' Sly said, 'this is my chance to get a cook for my kitchen, someone who will milk my cows for instance if I were at a horse fair in Galway . . . I'll have to be beside her until she gets used to working on my farm. Don't worry, Frances, I'll be back to my old ways before I am six months married.'

Frances gave an ignorant grunt and slapped him on the back.

Then Sly began to list the widow's virtues – that she did the finest churning in the district, that she could sew and knit and cook.

When Frances grew tired of listening to the praises of Lucinda Singleton, she turned on him sharply:

'God Almighty!' she exploded. 'One would think you were buying a mare. And how is she under the bedcovers? Maybe she has gone past it. That happens to women don't you know? You are rusty for lack of practice and she is worn out from the world and from the weather.'

54

'Listen to me, my good woman,' Sly turned on her, 'don't be discouraging me from what I have set before me. I have a plan in my head and, for the first time in my life, I'll have a woman at home before me who will put food on the table for me after a hard day's work.'

'Or after a day and night carousing in Langstrom's tavern,' she replied sharply. 'But then again, maybe it's the back of the brush across your back you'll get as soon as her feet get settled under your table.'

'I don't think that she is that kind of woman,' Sly informed her, 'and suppose she is, there is the width of the mountain to bring her to her senses. Now, if we have nothing further to discuss, I'll be shortening the road home.'

In a fit of temper, Sly threw back the drink she had stood him, jumped out of his chair and told the owner of the tavern to have a look out at the street so that he could leave to go home. When he did, Frances stood up.

'We'll shorten the road home for each other,' she said, standing drunkenly on her feet. 'I heard that there are tinkers camped a mile outside the town.'

The card players looked at each other and then at the two who were walking towards the door.

While they were on the road home, Frances never stopped trying to seduce Sly to come to her house so that they might 'stretch their thighs together' as she put it, but, although Sly had drink in him he put that kind of carousing on the long finger. Indeed, he wasn't about to spoil things when he was so close to getting a wife.

During the weeks and months that followed, Sly and Lucinda became more intimate as their courtship blossomed. Along with that, Sly was able to re-establish contact between Lucinda and her son. This was the quality Lucinda had been looking for in Sly's character that proved he would make a good husband.

When they had been courting regularly for six months, Sly felt the time had come to show her his house and farm of land.

On the first Sunday of August, 1828, Lucinda guided her horse and cart through Carlow town in the direction of Oldleighlin. The sky was clear and her journey was pleasant in the heat of the sun. She followed the directions Walter Sly had given her during the week. She saw the luscious green fields on both sides of the road. Sly owned the land on both sides from the King's road to the house and acre upon acre of bogland behind it on the other side if he was to be believed.

'The farm is three hundred acres between rough and good land. I will have the most butter to sell at Carlow fair,' Lucinda was thinking.

Walter was standing at the door happily waiting for her. He walked towards the gate of the haggard, took the left ring of the horse's headstall and guided him into the barn at the side of the house.

'Welcome to Oldleighlin, Lucinda,' he greeted her.

She jumped out of the cart as supple as a woman half her age. They both unyoked the horse and let him out to grass in the field behind the house. Sly walked in the door ahead of her and welcomed her warmly to 'Sly's Manor' as he called it.

Lucinda was very impressed with the cleanliness of the kitchen. It was fortunate that she had not seen it a few days earlier but, for the first time in his life, for this special occasion Sly spent two days cleaning and scrubbing.

'Sit down by the fire, my dear. Take off your shoes and warm your feet after your journey.' Sly began pleasantly putting the best sugawn chair in the house under her.

After they had been sitting for a few minutes, Lucinda couldn't but comment on the fine smell of food that was steaming in the big pot hanging on the crane over the fire.

'I'll wager that it's beef with white cabbage in the pot,' she ventured, leaning her head towards the pot.

'Better still,' Walter informed her, 'in the pot beside the beef and cabbage there are fine sweet turnips not to mention the stone of *Early Regent* potatoes in the pot in the embers. That is a new variety of potato that was brought here a few years ago. The soil in Ireland is very suitable for growing them. They are so dry and floury that one would need half a pound of butter with them in order to eat them.'

He lifted the cover of the pot and put it on the ground. Then he got a fork and stuck it up to the handle in the hunk of beef.

'Put a couple of plates on the table, Lucinda,' Sly said, 'because if this beef is over the fire any longer it will melt into the cabbage.'

Sly laid the plate of beef in the centre of the table and then put a coarse bag beside it. He took the pot of potatoes and turned it upside down on the bag.

'Ah, girl,' he beamed, 'look at those for potatoes. Every one of them bursting out of its skin.'

Lucinda had never seen Walter in such good humour as he was that Sunday. Without a doubt, it was not without reason. He had visited Constable Thomas Singleton the previous night. He told Thomas that he was going to propose to Lucinda. Along with giving Sly his blessing, he intimated to him that Lucinda would not refuse him.

When they had eaten, Sly cleared his throat, letting Lucinda know that he was about to put an important question to her. Of course, he had practised this twenty times during the week when he was about his work.

'Lucinda,' he began, 'It is more than six months since we became acquainted and we have been walking out together for about the same time. Neither of us is in the full bloom of youth and there is no chance that we will reach Tír na nÓg. You have been on your own for years and I have been too. I knew the evening when you gave out to me on the side of the street in Carlow that you were the woman for me. As the weeks and months went by and I was getting to know you, love for you blossomed in my heart. Look, without further ado, before I put my two feet in it and make a fool of myself, what I am trying to say is I would like you to marry me.'

Lucinda was like a shy young girl with her eyes fixed on the ground. She spent a minute thinking deeply. Sly was becoming restless waiting for a reply.

'Look,' he said in an attempt to put her at ease, 'I know that we would have a lot to discuss; we will have to come to an agreement about your house and land and many other matters . . . '

'That's exactly it,' Lucinda replied. 'I would be willing to marry you but, as you said, many arrangements will have to be made.'

'Oh, I understand that,' Sly assured her, 'but we could do that on the day of the wedding or a week afterwards. We will walk around my farm soon and you will see that you will be getting the better of the bargain as regards land.'

Lucinda stood her ground.

'I am too long on the road and too long in the tooth to buy a pig in a poke,' she countered. 'There is a long evening before us and we have nothing to do but settle things between us before nightfall. Then we can meet in Carlow town during the week and let an attorney make everything legal.'

By God, but Sly understood, on hearing this from Lucinda, that she was no fool. What she said took him unawares but that didn't discourage him. He knew that if the marriage didn't work out that a woman wouldn't get much justice in the courts.

'As regards the land,' Sly spoke with authority, 'I would be happy to make a will leaving it to you should I die before you. Against that you would sign your house and your few acres over to me. Then the best thing would be to let it out to pasture and put the money into this farm.'

'Yes, but what about my house? Will you be putting it on the market?' Lucinda questioned him with a doubt in her mind as to what Sly had said.

'You can bring your furniture and any personal belongings you have your heart set on to this house and, I suppose, after a while when you are properly settled in here, we could sell it,' Sly allowed.

Lucinda was in deep thought again.

'Sell my house?' she erupted. 'The house where I reared my child without a father's help and where I churned the best butter in the seven parishes on the hearthstone every season since my husband died?'

Sly realised that he had better back off at this point as he was playing with a strong-minded woman. He would have plenty of time to deal with minor matters after they were married.

'Sure if you have your heart set on that small felt house we'll leave it aside. It won't make any money without the land going with it,' Sly replied steadily.

'It is I who will be in charge of the churning and sale of the butter,' Lucinda insisted. 'I will have permission to spend some of the money on myself. Without a doubt, most of the money will go on the running of the house. I want to sell the butter on the side of the street just as I have done for more than thirty years.'

'Yes,' Sly assured her. 'Upon my word you will be in charge of the churning, the running of the house and milking the cows. Without a doubt, if the work should at any time become too heavy for you, we will get a servant girl or boy. At our age, we don't need slavery.'

When she heard this, Lucinda could not but be happy in her mind. She would have her own kitchen, control of the butter making and the freedom to spend some of the money.

'Isn't it a pity I didn't meet this man thirty years ago?' she thought to herself. She grew excited when Sly told her that they should go to the attorney as soon as possible.

'I'll be going to Carlow on Thursday selling my butter,' she informed him. 'Will you be able to meet me any time about mid-day, Walter?'

'I'll be going to town the same day,' Sly told her. 'I'll meet you at the attorney's office at three o'clock.'

After Lucinda had taken the ware from the table, put them in a dish of water and cleaned and wiped the table, she sat on a chair by the fire. Sly sat beside her and reddened his pipe with a coal from the fire. He was totally at ease.

'When I have finished my smoke, we will walk around the farm,' he suggested.

They walked out the back door and through the broken bog to the top of a low hill where they had a fine view of the countryside all around. The way Sly was casting his eyes around, one would be forgiven for thinking that this was his first trip to the top of the hill.

'Look down there in the direction of Carlow town,' he boasted as he stretched himself, 'and east towards the thatched house . . . then west to the big glen . . . I own every acre of it. Between commonage and land there are more than three hundred acres and perhaps in a few years a few holdings will be added to it.'

Lucinda saw the glint of the landlord in his eyes but she let it go without saying a word. She supposed it wasn't a bad thing in a man to have a desire for land.

Lucinda Singleton couldn't but be satisfied in her mind as she guided her horse home from Oldleighlin that evening. There

Maidhc Dainín Ó Sé

would be an end to her poverty not to mention her fear of putting a ha'penny astray. She would be able to buy a new pair of shoes and a shawl at least every other year instead of resoling old shoes whose uppers and seams were rotten from cowdung and milk that spilled from the pails. She imagined she would have a good life as soon as she was married and settled in Walter's farm. Yes, and the *snooties* who sold their butter on the side of the street and were looking down on the widow wouldn't be able to do so any longer.

She visited her son and his wife briefly before she left Bilboa to strengthen the friendship Walter Sly had re-established between them. But she didn't spend too long in their company as night was falling. In those days a woman travelling on her own wouldn't be safe on the King's road. At that time stories were going around that a woman who was walking home on her own from a neighbour's house was viciously attacked. The poor woman ended up in the lunatic asylum as a result. Yes, and it wasn't the fairies who attacked her.

When Lucinda reached home she unyoked the horse and let him out in the field. There was so much running through her mind that she almost forgot to milk her two cows.

'Anyone would think that I'm only an eighteen-year-old the way my head is spinning,' she thought to herself as she loosened the spancel from the second cow's legs. The day's events were still going around in her mind.

Because there was a nature of frost in the north wind, she lit the fire. She would get no sleep until she went over in her mind her arrangement with Walter Sly. Suddenly she began to have doubts.

62

Was she doing the right thing? She had spent most of her life working her few acres on her own without anybody to tell her 'do this' or 'do that'. In a short time she would be married and she would be answerable for two.

Little by little the fire lit up until it threw light on the whole kitchen. Lucinda sat looking into the heart of the fire, her mind still on Walter Sly's farm and question after question worrying her. Oh! She had a long dark road ahead of her. It wasn't too late to pull back from the brink but, then again, would she end up a cantankerous, tormented old woman sitting on her own in the corner with nobody to look after her? Contact had been re-established between herself and her son thanks to Walter Sly. The blaze of the fire was a help to her, she felt. If it did nothing else, it put her mind at ease and, at the end of the night before she put her head on the pillow, she had decided that she would take a chance on marrying Walter Sly.

# Chapter Six

Lucinda Singleton spent the first three days of the following week doing the usual household chores and working on the farm. She baked twenty cakes of bread for the market on Thursday and because she had done the churning on the previous Saturday, she churned more during the day on the Wednesday. That took the edge from the strange thoughts that were running through her mind since the previous Sunday's events. On the Monday, she was saying to herself that she still had three days to accept or reject his offer although she had given Walter Sly to understand that the match was made. Matters hadn't quite come to a head by that Tuesday. But, when she sat in front of her turf fire on the Wednesday evening, when all the work was done and with nothing before her but her fateful day, she was both frightened and excited. She was sitting in her own comfortable corner independent of husband or government. But would things be like that after she married? 'Oh! God direct me on the right road in my time of need,' she prayed. Then, shaking herself, she said: 'I will always have my own little house here.'

She spent the whole night weighing up her situation. 'I'll go ahead with the wedding,' she would determine one minute, and, a little while later, she'd think, 'am I gone completely astray in my head?' The more she worried about it, the more confused she became. She tried to divert her thoughts, but in a moment they would have returned to the same old story again. It was getting late in the night and still she could get no proper sleep. If she didn't get at least eight hours' sleep, neither her mind nor her body would function properly the following day. And, perhaps, one of the most important days of her life was staring her in the face.

She got up, put a mug of milk into a saucepan and laid it on a few coals on the side of the fire. A saucepan of hot milk would put her to sleep any time she was troubled in her mind. When the milk was hot, she cut a hunk of wheaten bread and sat down again on the chair in front of the fire. First she ate a bite of bread and followed it with a mouthful of milk. What with the heat of the fire and the hot milk, Lucinda began to relax. 'Right, Lucinda,' she determined, 'put your head on the pillow before the night's sleep completely evades you.' She banked up the fire and returned to bed. She was barely a few minutes on her back when she fell into a deep sleep. She spent the entire night dreaming: her wedding to Walter Sly caused her nightmares that night.

When Lucinda woke the following morning she was in a cold sweat. She was as tired waking up as she was when she went to bed the previous night. Every bone in her body was weary as if she had just put in a hard day's work. After she had milked her two cows, skimmed the cream from the previous day's milk and cleaned and scalded the dishes she poured the morning's milk into the dishes. Just then she found herself getting hungry. She took a handful of potatoes that were roasting in the ashes of the fire and put them on a plate on the table. She satisfied her appetite as usual with a bowl of buttermilk along with the potatoes. She put Sly and the attorney to the back of her mind until the horse was harnessed and her bread and butter were secured in the cart. She jumped into the front of the cart and guided the horse down the King's road in the direction of Carlow town . . .

When Lucinda had found the stand she had stored in one of Langstrom's sheds, she stood it on the side of the street as usual. She was a couple of minutes earlier than the other women. She tied her horse to an iron ring that was on the side of the street and put an armful of hay under his head. She was waiting for her usual customers who came for their choice of the twenty fresh cakes of bread not to mention her butter that was in such high demand. Lucinda wanted to be finished early that day more than any other.

When she had a few moments to herself, she would look down the street expecting that she would see Walter Sly. By the time she had sold her last cake of bread, the sun was high in the sky. Just as she was dismantling her stand to store it in the shed at the back of Langstrom's tavern, she caught sight of Walter Sly on horseback, a tall black hat on his head; he was dressed in an expensive suit from the tailors. 'Oh! He is as well turned out as the Duke of Leinster,' Lucinda was thinking excitedly. She looked then at the other women who were standing at their stalls down the street. Like Lucinda, they, too, had their eyes on the big man on horseback.

Lucinda put a pack she had specially made on her horse's head with a fist of oats in it. She was making sure that he would stay quiet while she and Walter were attending to their business in the attorney's.

Walter guided his horse into Langstrom's stable and then walked cheerfully over in Lucinda's direction.

'Have you everything sold?' he asked her.

She looked at him with affection.

'If you were ten minutes earlier, you would have to wait,' she informed him.

'Right so, we have urgent matters to attend to,' Sly said with authority.

They walked down the street towards the attorney's office. The women who were selling at their stalls gathered in twos and threes whispering and peering inquisitively at the two who were walking close together quickly down the street.

Just as they were turning in the attorney's entrance, the woman who was in charge of the stand in front of the door spoke:

'Whatever business you have, or bargain you have made with that tramp, it won't be long before you regret it, my good woman,' she spat.

Sly turned violently.

'When you go home this evening,' he retorted, 'take a shovel in your hand and give your husband a couple of belts of it across his back. Maybe he might get up off his arse and do some work.'

'At least he isn't running poor people off their land,' she replied. 'But, I promise you, the earth in the field between us will turn to limestone before your name will be on it, Walter Sly.' Lucinda stood inside the door and looked hard at him.

'What was that woman out there talking about?' she demanded.

'Ah! Don't worry about that old hag,' he reassured her. 'She is a neighbour of mine whose husband came to me in service when he had nothing to do on his own few acres. And what a lazy lout he was. If he wasn't lying asleep in the cow's stall, the layabout would be stretched in the middle of the bog, his two legs sticking out from the heather and turf to be footed all around him.'

Walter Sly knocked gently on the door of the office.

'Come in,' said a soft voice from inside.

Sly opened the door and beckoned Lucinda to enter before him. There were two chairs beside a table and a small, tidy man seated behind it.

'Welcome,' he greeted them. 'Is this the young woman you were talking about, Walter?'

When Lucinda heard this she had to laugh.

'It's a long time since I was called a young woman,' she said shyly.

'Don't be so hard on yourself,' the attorney replied. 'You are still a fine woman. If you were not, the finest of men and the richest farmer in the area would not be looking for your hand in marriage. Yes, now, sit you both down and we will get matters underway. My name is John Burke. I expect that you will have matters arranged between yourselves. If you have we should have no delay.'

'Yes, we have, but we have nothing put on paper,' Sly informed him.

'That is why you have come to me,' Burke replied. 'Now, I shall begin with you, Lucinda. Tell me what arrangement you have come to with Walter Sly. Take your time and think clearly about what you have to say because when you have signed this paper and the official seal is on it, it will have the force of law.'

Lucinda spent a minute in deep thought before she began to speak. She looked at Walter and in those few seconds the thought struck her that she would be better not to proceed. But the life of a healthy person is eighty years and she was not far off her last two decades.

'Walter and I have decided to rent my land for grazing and to put the rent money into the farm in Oldleighlin, then I will do the churning and sell the butter in Carlow town, a job I'm well used to. I will help with the milking of the cows and, if I have time, other farm work as well. I will put up three meals a day on the table for him. The animals on my holding will be brought to Oldleighlin and they will be part of the stock on the land there. I will do my duty as a faithful partner in marriage and he will do likewise. On those conditions he will have to put in his will that if anything were to happen to him, for instance if he were to die suddenly – God between us and all harm – that the farm will be mine. But the farm will remain in his name as long as he is alive. That is my part of the bargain. Along with that, my farm will be put in Walter's name as a dowry,' Lucinda finished, glad that that much was over.

The attorney looked at Sly.

'Is that your understanding, Walter,' he asked him, 'or is there

something you want to add to it or maybe make some correc-
tions?'

Sly spent a little while in thought.

'That is exactly what we have agreed,' he said quietly.

'All right,' the attorney continued. 'You may go out in town for
an hour or so. That will afford me an opportunity to draw up the
document and you both can read and sign it on your return. I will
keep it under lock and key in the safe and it will be there in the
event of any disagreement later on.'

Lucinda felt much better leaving the office than she did on
going in. It wouldn't be long before the bargain was sealed and in
the attorney's safe. Now all that was to be done was to go to the
minister to solemnise the marriage and she would have a happy
and contented life from then on.

'I have a couple of hunks of bread in a bag in my cart and a bottle of this morning's buttermilk,' Lucinda told Walter. 'Will you
come and eat with me? We will have to wait for an hour for the
attorney to prepare his paper.'

'I have some business in town,' Sly lied. 'I'll meet you here in an
hour.' Lucinda believed him. What was in Sly's head was to have a
word in private with the attorney. When Lucinda had gone out of
sight, he turned in to the office again.

'Excuse me,' Sly began, 'but could you add one more thing to
the document – that if Lucinda doesn't discharge her duties properly I can change my will?'

'There is no need,' the attorney informed him. 'You have a right
to do that without putting anything in writing. But you will have

to make a will soon because, what with the document I am currently putting together, if any accident should befall you, everything would be null and void if Lucinda is not mentioned in your will. You may alter your will at any time in the future. Married women don't understand this, but they have little power when it comes to having a claim on land or possession of a house because if the holding was originally the husband's, he puts his wife's name in his will. The husband can change his will during their marriage and the wife will not get even what she brought with her as a dowry the day they married.'

'I understand,' said Sly.

He put a half sovereign in the attorney's coat pocket.

'Have a drink on me later on,' Sly said, winking at the attorney.

Sly walked out the door with a smile on his face.

The glass of whiskey he had in Langstrom's a few minutes later went down well. He met some of his old cronies who wanted to know why he hadn't been seen much in the taverns for over six months.

'Oh! I got sense,' he replied and left it at that.

He kept an eye on the clock. He didn't want to make any mistake until they were safely married and Lucinda was under his roof for some time.

Sly and Lucinda were both going in the attorney's door at virtually the same time.

'Did you get your business done?' Lucinda asked him.

'I did,' Sly lied. 'There was a few pounds coming to me from a man who bought a horse from me. We had a drop of whiskey in

Langstrom's to seal the bargain.'

'Hum,' was all Lucinda said, pretending to be disgusted and letting him know that she still remembered the day they first met on the side of the street.

'I understand that you don't like drink,' Sly offered, 'but believe me I had too much to drink the first time we met. That won't happen again.'

'I hope not,' Lucinda warned him.

The attorney offered the document to Lucinda.

'Read what is written in this document,' he advised her, 'and, if you are satisfied that everything is in order, sign your name or make your mark where I have made a cross.'

Lucinda pretended to read the document, but she had had little education in her youth. Then she took the pen in her hand and signed it. Sly signed it after her without so much as reading one sentence. They thanked the attorney and walked towards the door. When they were out on the street they both stopped. Sly was first to speak.

'Yes, now,' he cleared this throat, 'that's the most important thing discussed and set right. I suppose we should go to the minister and fix a date for the wedding.'

'We should,' Lucinda agreed. 'And we each will have to get a witness. I'll ask my next-door neighbour, Mary Joy. She is a member of the Church of Ireland like myself.'

'I'll ask your son, Thomas,' Sly informed her. 'All my neighbours in Oldleighlin are Catholics and they hate anybody sympathetic to the Crown. Isn't it usual for the couple to tie the knot in the woman's local church?'

'That's right,' Lucinda replied.

'You can go to the minister and fix a date and I will see you at the market next Thursday,' Sly said.

'And what will happen if the date doesn't suit you?' Lucinda questioned him.

'Any date will suit me,' Sly assured her.

'Right,' Lucinda smiled. 'I'll be shortening the road home and I will have news for you on Thursday. We won't make with a big day's drinking out of it, Walter Sly, but maybe the four of us will have a few quiet drinks after the wedding. We're too long in the tooth for that.'

Sly ripped the reins for her and helped her into the cart, then he drew a swipe of his crop across the horse's flank and he trotted off down the road.

Sly stood until Lucinda and her horse had disappeared from sight at the bottom of the street. 'A good day's work,' he was thinking to himself. Then he headed for Langstrom's . . .

Lucinda Singleton and Walter Sly were married on the third Saturday of August, 1831. There were very few people in the church apart from Thomas Singleton and Mary Joy who were standing with the couple and half a dozen or so of Lucinda's neighbours who were curious about what kind of man she was marrying. It was a simple service without even a flower on the altar. The service began on the stroke of midday. They were standing outside the church door half an hour later, a newly married couple.

They travelled by horse and trap to Carlow town where there

was a meal waiting for them in Fitzgerald's Hotel. Their meal was boiled pork with potatoes, green cabbage and turnips. Lucinda was very impressed as few people would have had such fare before them in those times.

Thomas did most of the talking during the meal, telling the other three how difficult a policeman's life had become during the previous few years. The tenants of smallholdings in the west of the county were getting agitated and threatening the landlords because their rent was rising every year. According to the tenants, with every improvement they made on their holdings the landlords would raise their rent a shilling or two every quarter. If a family was being evicted from their land, the farmers of the parish would gather outside that family's house and chase off the bailiffs. It was the policemen's lot then to evict the family. That gave rise to bad feelings between the police and the ordinary people.

'There is one cure for those criminals,' Sly blurted out ignorantly. 'The government should bring in the army and any farmer who refuses to leave his holding should be shot.' On hearing this statement from Sly, Mary Joy almost choked on the meat she was chewing.

'Perhaps,' she suggested, 'if the landlords reduced the rent on smallholdings by half, the poor creatures wouldn't have to come together and break the law.'

Thomas cleared his throat vigorously but Sly didn't take the hint.

'The dogs of the town know what the small farmers around here are up to,' Sly continued. 'Aren't most of them Catholics and don't they want to get rid of the Empire from this island? Yes, and if that happens they'll get rid of all the Protestants.'

Just then Sly realised that Lucinda had a smallholding.

'It's the Catholics I'm talking about, Lucinda,' he said by way of appeasing her. 'You know that.'

'You're saying that because I'm a Protestant and a tenant on a smallholding, that it doesn't concern me,' she retorted. 'Listen now. The British government doesn't care about what God any of us have as long as we pay our rent to the landlords every quarter.'

They had almost finished their meal and it was time to celebrate the wedding. Sly beckoned to the waitress to bring out four glasses and the bottle of whiskey he had left with the hoteliers when he had made the reservation for the meal. The four of them drank to each other's health and then they toasted the newly married couple and wished them a long and happy life together.

# Chapter Seven

No sooner was Lucinda out of the bed the morning after the wedding than she hung a skillet on the crook over the fire. She would make a bowl of porridge for her husband that would stick to his ribs and get him through the day's work, a handful of potatoes and a mug of milk after that and a hunk of the wheaten bread she had baked the previous day. 'There is nothing like a bowl of porridge made from cows' milk,' she thought to herself. She put two eggs boiling on the coals at the side of the fire.

Lucinda had the breakfast on the table before Walter rose. He entered the room stretching himself like a man who had had a good night's sleep.

'Eat your breakfast before we milk the cows,' Lucinda suggested, pointing to the substantial breakfast that was laid out at the head of the table.

When they both were seated comfortably, Walter spoke:

'What have you planned to do today, Lucinda?'

Lucinda thought for a minute.

'Because yesterday was our wedding day, there is no need for us to go to church two days in a row,' she replied.

'Oh yes, today is Sunday,' Sly observed.

'I was examining the churn at the bottom of the house,' Lucinda continued. 'It looks like the hoops are rusty and could burst when it is full of cream.'

'I intended to buy a new churn,' Sly told her, 'but you know, a man puts everything on the long finger until the worst happens.'

'Listen,' Lucinda suggested, 'we will milk the cows and while we have the time we could bring my own churn over from my house. It is almost new. Yes, and while we are there, I might as well harness my horse. With two horses we will be able to transport my furniture and any other personal belongings over here. We could drive my two cows before us also.'

Sly's heart rose when she mentioned that they could bring the two cows to Oldleighlin and he agreed that Sunday was the right day to do it. According to him, the sooner she broke her ties with her old homestead the better because he intended to sell her house and land together when Lucinda was settled in Oldleighlin. But he would not reveal to her what was in his mind just yet.

It was late that Sunday evening when Walter and Lucinda Sly guided their two horses down the boreen towards their house. Both carts were piled up back to the heels and to the top of the rails. She even brought her own bed. Sly was breathless from trying to drive the two cows on the long road home without any chance of stopping at Langstrom's to relax and quench his thirst, but he considered it too early in the marriage to be causing ripples when they hadn't yet gotten to know each other properly.

He would have another day!

When they had moved the furniture into the house, while they were unyoking the horses, Lucinda surprised Walter.

'As soon as we have the cows milked,' she told him, 'why don't you saddle the white mare? She is out in pasture all day. Have a few drinks in Carlow town. You have it well earned.'

Sly's heart rose when he heard that. But Lucinda added:

'And don't let it be bright morning when you come home.'

When Walter Sly had stabled his horse in Langstrom's stables, he walked to the front door of the tavern. The moon was almost full and the sky was clear. He looked over and back in case any policeman was patrolling the street as they usually did on Sunday nights. There was neither human nor spirit to be seen nor sound to be heard in any direction. He knocked gently on the door. It wasn't long before he heard the bolt being drawn inside. The door opened by two inches.

'Walter,' a voice whispered, 'come in quickly. A new policeman has come to town and he has nothing better to do but march up and down the street listening at every tavern door.'

There were only five people drinking inside and Walter knew every one of them.

'How is it that none of you are playing cards?' Sly wanted to know.

'Because Langstrom won't let us play until he finds out what kind of policeman this stranger is that has come to town,' John Moore, one of the town's shopkeepers, answered him.

Suddenly he looked at Sly.

'Was I dreaming,' he asked him, 'or is it true that you got married yesterday?'

On hearing this, the other four customers finished their drinks as it was the custom that a newly married man would stand to his friends particularly if there was no wedding feast at his house.

'Ah here!' Sly instructed the man of the house. 'Fill them a drink and have one yourself. I knew I wouldn't get away easily with this.'

'Do we know the woman you married?' Francis Ware, a small, useless article who had a habit of sticking his nose in other people's business, enquired.

'Lucinda Singleton is her name,' Sly informed him. 'A widow who spent her life working hard. We are both nearly the same age. She is well used to farm work and if it gets lonely up there on the side of the hill during the long winter nights when I am at home, she will be company for me.'

'Isn't she the one the women at the market call the hag with the butter?' Ware persisted.

Well, when Sly heard the insult coming from Ware's mouth, he caught him by the windpipe and shoved him into the corner. He jumped on him like a fox would jump on a hen. It took three customers as well as the owner to pull Sly off him.

When Sly had cooled down somewhat, the three customers put him sitting at the bottom of the counter as far as possible from Francis Ware, who was fit to shit in his pants so afraid was he that Sly would kill him.

'Listen, Walter,' Ware pleaded. 'It wasn't out of badness I said it but it was my own wife who told me.'

'Will I include him in the round?' Langstrom asked Sly when everybody was seated on their stools again.

'Fill the drink,' Sly ordered him, 'and don't leave anybody out.'

Sly drank his fill of whiskey that night. But he didn't stay too late. He had to mend ditches between his land and Connors's. Connors had come complaining about his horses three times in the space of a month.

When Walter Sly awoke the following morning, his breakfast was on the table for him and Lucinda was churning at the bottom of the kitchen. She threw a hard eye in his direction.

'You had a good drop in when you came home last night,' she began. 'You spent the night shouting in a nightmare. I didn't sleep a wink because you were tossing and turning beside me. I left you in bed this morning, I milked the cows and your breakfast is on the table. It doesn't bother me if you have a few drinks. But if you come home with too much to drink there will be no peace between us.'

Sly didn't open his mouth but he was grinding his teeth with rage. It was too early in their marriage to be arguing. He sat at the table and ate his breakfast. He got up from the table without a word. As he was going out, he stopped at the door and spoke in a harsh voice:

'I'm going to mend the ditches,' he said, 'in order to keep the neighbours from my door. I'll be home early in the evening.'

'I'll bake a couple of cakes for the market,' Lucinda replied, letting him know that she wouldn't be idle.

The marriage worked well for the first couple of months as Walter Sly was drinking very little. As well as that he went only to the horse fairs that were nearby so that he could be home in time for milking the cows. But he had other plans. He was failing to get anyone to lease the grazing of Lucinda's holding. As well as that nobody had any interest in leasing her house. One day he was in Carlow while Lucinda was selling her butter and bread on the side of the street. Walter went across to the tavern for a drink. Because autumn was over and the cold of winter was in the wind blowing from the north, he knew that Lucinda wouldn't be long selling what little butter she had. The cows were heavy in calf and were almost dry.

'Give me two small whiskies in the one glass,' Sly ordered, shaking himself with the cold.

Nobody was in the tavern only himself and the owner.

'Do you know,' Langstrom began, 'since there are only the two of us here, I'll have a dram with you. Leave your money in your pocket, Walter. You have been a good customer down through the years.'

Langstrom never stood to anybody without getting his own back in one way or another. He filled their glasses a second time and drew up his stool closer to Walter.

'Walter,' he enquired, 'did you let the grazing of Lucinda's farm yet?'

'I didn't even have an enquiry,' Walter lamented. 'There's a fine top of grass and not an animal grazing it this past year. It is my opinion that the holding is too small not to mention that it is too far from my farm at home. Do you know anybody who would be interested in buying the house and the holding together?'

'I thought you promised Lucinda that it would be let,' Langstrom ventured.

'That's what I planned but nobody is interested in it,' Sly told him. 'I'd sell the house and land if I got a decent offer.'

That is exactly what Langstrom wanted to hear. Sly didn't know that Langstrom had come into possession of a piece of land. His uncle had died and left fifty acres to him in his will.

'What kind of money would you want for the house and land together?' Langstrom queried. 'And take it from me that it should be reasonable.'

Sly drank a mouthful of whiskey and looked at Langstrom.

'Because it is so far from my own holding I'd sell it for a hundred and twenty pounds,' Sly offered.

When he heard that, Langstrom jumped from his stool.

'I thought you were anxious to sell it,' he thundered. 'For the money you are asking, I could buy half the land around the town of Tullow.'

Sly thought for a moment.

'Look,' he said, 'you can have it for a hundred, but I will have to get the money into my hand. Christ, how could I face Lucinda and tell her that I didn't get a decent price for the farm where she made her living for forty-odd years in bad times?'

'All right,' Langstrom agreed. 'But you will have to give me five pounds luck.'

'Three pounds,' Sly offered.

'It's a bargain,' Langstrom said.

They agreed on the spot that they would go to the attorney to seal the bargain. They drank their whiskey and Langstrom stood another round before he shut the door behind them and both of them walked down the street to the attorney's office. John Burke was seated in his chair, busily poring over documents when the two walked in. Within a minute he raised his eyes from the papers in front of him.

'Ah, God be with you, men,' he welcomed them. 'And what brings you to an attorney's office this cold winter's day?'

'Do you remember the holding my wife gave me as a dowry before we married?' Sly began.

'Oh yes,' the lawyer replied, 'have you found somebody to rent it from you?'

'Well,' Sly stuttered, 'the place isn't being let. I have sold house and land to Mister Langstrom.'

'Oh,' the lawyer continued, 'has your wife changed her mind? I thought she wanted to lease it for grazing rather than sell it.'

'I tried my best to lease it and honour my wife's wishes but I failed,' Sly informed him. 'It isn't every day a buyer comes along. Is it in the marriage agreement that I can't sell it?'

'There's nothing legally binding written down but I thought that you both had agreed to hold on to the house and farm,' the lawyer reminded him.

'When we said that, neither of us knew how difficult it is to lease land,' Sly insisted.

'Look, Walter,' the attorney looked him in the eye. 'It's none of my business. The land is legally in your name. Right so, gentlemen, we'll get down to business because I have enough to do besides dawdling with two men who have time to waste.'

No two in the town of Carlow were more satisfied in their minds than John Langstrom and Walter Sly that cold Thursday in winter: Langstrom had bought the land he wanted at a reasonable price and Sly had gotten rid of the millstone around his neck. Yes, and dry cash in his pocket for the horse fair in Ballinasloe. But how would he tell Lucinda? Well, he need not break the news until after the Ballinasloe fair. He could be complaining little by little to her how difficult it was to do any work on land so far from the main farm.

Walter Sly was making his way to the tavern along with Langstrom in order to collect his money. Sly was goggle-eyed when he saw Langstrom counting from a wad of notes that he brought down from one of the upstairs rooms.

'In the name of God, John, wouldn't your money be safer in a bank than under your bed?' Sly reproached him.

Langstrom looked at Sly and the stamp of the rogue was on his forehead. 'I like to lay it out on the table now and then,' he said, 'and, since you mentioned it, I don't trust strangers.'

Sly handed the three pounds luck money to Langstrom who threw a pound on the bar counter.

'We'll drink the pound to celebrate the bargain,' he insisted.

'I'll have one more drink,' Sly replied, 'but I'll have to go home with Lucinda.'

'Yes!' Langstrom smiled. 'We know who wears the trousers in your house.'

Sly wasn't a man to let it be known that he would be led and said by a woman.

'All right so,' he retorted, 'since you are buying, fill the glasses.'

Lucinda finished her business at the market and harnessed the horse. She spent some time waiting for Walter and when he wasn't coming to her she had a good idea where she would find him. She tied the horse to the ring and hurried towards the tavern. The two were still drinking Langstrom's pound. Lucinda stood at the threshold.

'Walter,' she said firmly, 'the horse is harnessed and it's time to go home.'

Sly almost choked on his whiskey he got such a fright.

'I'll be straight out to you. Release the reins,' he said in order to calm the situation.

He hurried out of the tavern and jumped into the front of the cart. Neither of them spoke on the long road home.

Strange thoughts were running through Lucinda's mind: that whatever affection was between herself and Walter at first was beginning to wane. He was becoming more abusive by the day and insulted her in every move she made. The day before the fair in Ballinasloe he told her for the first time that she was expecting too much from the marriage.

After supper that evening he sat by the fire, took off his shoes and laid them at his feet. Lucinda was washing the ware in a dish at the bottom of the table.

'You have been very quiet there for a while,' Sly said to her. 'Is there something bothering you?'

'There is,' she told him. 'Your drinking has gone to the dogs; you come home unable to get off your horse or walk in the door without stumbling and then you snore, you give every hop in the bed not to mention farting until bright morning . . . You have no thought for the desires of your wife in bed beside you. I am a woman who has desires and all you do is satisfy your own. As well as that, you haven't been doing your fair share of the farm work for a while. That is not the bargain we made before we married.'

Sly straightened himself in the chair with a snarl.

'Neither of us will be able to gain anything from the farm until next spring. As soon as the cows are calving, I'll hire a servant boy or girl for you who will do the heavy work.'

Lucinda put down the ware she was drying and looked at him with an odd stare.

'You'll get a servant girl or boy and what will you be doing?' she demanded. 'Scratching your backside in the taverns in Carlow town.'

'My good woman,' Sly informed her, 'I will be doing what I should have been doing for the past year instead of attending to you and trying to satisfy you. I'll be selling and buying horses and, to do that, I'll be travelling far from home to the fairs.'

'There are more than two hundred acres around the house that need to be improved,' she reminded him. 'There are boundary ditches to be repaired, potatoes still in the earth, winter is upon us and we're in danger of frost that would spoil all the potatoes.'

Yes! It took her almost a year to get that much off her chest. It had come to war between them.

Walter Sly spent some time reflecting on what Lucinda had said and thinking to himself, was this the same small, mild-mannered woman he walked out with for half a year and then married.

'Sooner or later I'll have to show her where the woman's place is in this house,' he was thinking. It was on the tip of his tongue to tell her that it would be better for her to mind the house she was living in as she had no other from the time her own house and farm were sold and he had the money in his pocket intending to buy twenty horses on the strength of it. But he held his tongue on this occasion. He didn't want to go to the fair with bad blood between them. He considered he had said enough for the time being. He had his whole life to control her when he was at home.

After a while when their anger had subsided a little, and Lucinda was seated by the fire knitting, Sly broke the silence.

'I'm going to the horse fair in Ballinasloe tomorrow,' he told her. 'I'll be gone for three or four days. Do you think you can do the farm work without me?'

Lucinda raised her head and cast a lethal eye in his direction.

'Off you go to the fair. There is nothing to be done only to dig the potatoes,' she replied.

'I hired our neighbour, Michael Connors, and he told me he will begin digging the potatoes next Monday,' he said. 'His two boys can pick them. I told him to put them in a pit in the field.'

When Lucinda heard that, it eased her a little. 'Go to the fair,' she told him, 'and buy your foals or horses but don't come home blind drunk. I don't mind a few drinks but if you are drunk stay outside in the stable until you come to your senses.'

Walter didn't reply but looked into the heart of the fire pretending that he didn't hear a word.

Sly had an early breakfast the following morning. After he had shaved himself, he dressed in his Sunday clothes and put on a tall black hat he got as a present from a buyer of horses a year previously. It was the same hat that sealed the deal when he was buying the black foal he still had and that he would ride to the fair. He thought that good luck would go hand-in-hand with the hat and the horse. Sly was full of superstition.

When he had washed and shaved, put on his shoes and leather gaiters up to his knees, he took his riding crop that was on top of the dresser and slapped his left gaiter with it. Lucinda, who was going through the door having given mess to the hens, got such a fright she almost dropped the empty dish.

Sly raised his hat as he was going past her as a sign that he was leaving. Lucinda followed him as far as the door and watched him jumping on the horse's back and after he had prodded the horse with his crop he went trotting down the boreen and out of sight.

'The Devil go with you and your horse,' Lucinda said beneath her breath. 'Why did I marry that scamp and not stay in my own house? Yes, and if he continues drinking constantly, I won't put up with it much longer.'

Because it was the month of November, there were only two cows to be milked and they would have been dry as well only they had slung their calves and it was late in the autumn when they were bulled again.

The thought struck her that she should travel to her old house and visit Mary Joy. If she left immediately, she would be back home before nightfall. Even though she was a fast walker it would take most of the morning and up to lunchtime before she reached Mary's house a couple of miles from the town of Tullow.

She put on her Sunday shoes she had bought for her wedding and a black shawl. Down the boreen she went, her heart as light as the thrush singing from the top of a furze bush. Since it was Friday, Carlow town was reasonably busy. Pig farmers sold their bonhams and fat pigs there every Friday. It was a long walk south-east to Tullow and Lucinda was regretting that she didn't bring the horse.

By the time she reached the top of the boreen that led to her own house she had to loosen the thongs of her shoes. She sat on the side of the boundary ditch between her farm and the Joys'. She drew a long breath of relief, her head raised in the direction of the sky so that she could fill her lungs with the fresh air of her home. Then she cast her eye over the ditch at her farm and, down in a corner of a field, her own felt-covered house.

'How is it that there is smoke coming from the chimney?' she wondered. She forgot the thongs of her shoes, jumped to her feet and hurried in the direction of her house.

'Walter didn't tell me that the house was let,' she said as she hurried towards the door. She raised the latch and, without knocking, opened the door.

Who should be sitting on a settle at the side of the kitchen in front of her? Langstrom, the tavern keeper from Carlow. He got such a fright when the door opened so suddenly that he nearly fell off the settle. Lucinda looked at him for a few seconds.

'Do you mind telling me what you are doing in my house?' she demanded. By this time she was frothing at the mouth with venom.

Langstrom stood in the middle of the floor.

'Didn't Walter tell you that I bought the house and land from him?' he answered.

Lucinda walked in circles around the kitchen.

'Are you sure that you haven't just leased it?' she demanded again.

'Oh no!' Langstrom retorted. 'I had my eye on this place since my uncle left me the farm down the road in his will.'

'Oh that bastard Sly,' Lucinda swore. 'I made a bad bargain. I told him to let the land and, if possible, to rent the house. The attorney was present when I put it to Walter. And wasn't it he who promised me faithfully that that is how it would be.'

Langstrom looked at her with a strange look.

'The attorney has no such thing in writing,' he informed her.

'You are right about that,' Lucinda agreed, 'but I can tell you that my name is in the will he made before that same attorney. If that is the kind of man I married, well two can play at that game. To satisfy my curiosity, how much money did you give him for the farm and house together?'

Langstrom looked at Lucinda, then down at the floor.

'One hundred pounds outright and I got three pounds luck,' he told her.

'Wasn't it nice of him?' Lucinda said. 'The house and land together are worth at least two hundred pounds particularly as the one who was buying it has a farm beside them.'

'Maybe he didn't know that I had been willed a farm nearby,' Langstrom countered.

'The stump of a fool,' Lucinda thundered. 'What came over me to marry him?'

Lucinda rushed out and slammed the door after her. She was talking to herself on the way to Mary Joy's house. Never in her life had she been betrayed like this . . . But deceit catches up with the deceiver.

Mary welcomed her friend heartily.

'Sit down, Lucinda,' she greeted her, 'and tell me all about your life in Oldleighlin – your purse full and women attending to you every time you ring the bell.'

Lucinda sat, tired and weary, on the settle.

'Oh, Mary, my dear,' she sighed, 'the opposite is the case. I am married to an old codger who has no respect for women. Don't be talking about him in bed – he's useless. He thinks women were put into the world to be servants to men and to do the housework and farm work as well.'

Mary stood in front of her staring at her in surprise.

'Ah, tell the truth,' she laughed. 'He is noted for his deeds under the covers.'

'God's honest truth,' Lucinda told her, 'he throws his leg over me, in and out and plups! He stretches himself backwards and in a short time he is snoring.'

'You don't say it,' Mary said in disbelief. 'He had a reputation once for . . . oh, excuse me, you are married to him.'

'Out with it, Mary, my dear,' Lucinda insisted. 'I was told after I married him that there wasn't a tinker woman going the road that he hadn't mounted. To give Mary Walsh her due, she gave me that information when she heard I was walking out with him but a few other women who were selling butter on the side of the street told me it wasn't true. Now they are all saying it.'

'Give him a chance,' Mary advised her. 'Maybe it is lack of practice. Listen! I was hanging out clothes on a bush a little while ago. I saw smoke coming from your chimney. I knew then that you had come to visit your old home.'

There was silence for a few seconds. Then Lucinda cleared her throat.

'It wasn't I who put down that fire,' she told her. 'Walter sold my house and land without even telling me.'

Lucinda burst out crying and the two women put their arms around one another.

'God save us,' Mary comforted her, 'but how did he manage to sell the house and land? Didn't he have to get your permission to do that?'

'I had put the house and land in Walter's name, you know, as a dowry for our wedding,' Lucinda informed her.

'Here,' said Mary, 'have a cup of milk.'

The two women spent a couple of hours going over everything

that happened to Lucinda since she left her home. They would not see each other again until the beginning of spring as Mary's cows were dry for a month. Mary wouldn't be at the fair again until the end of January. Their chat brought some relief to Lucinda. Walter would be at the fair for three days and she would be alone with her thoughts and would have time to think deeply about her married life in the years that were before her. She would have to confront Walter as soon as he came home in order to clear the air. Would there be peace between them or would it be out and out war? But Lucinda wasn't about to spend her remaining years as a slave to a blackguard, attending to him every time he whistled. 'I won't be any man's servant,' she vowed to herself.

# Chapter Eight

Late in the evening of the following Tuesday, Lucinda was sitting beside a blazing turf fire she had lit. She was finishing the second of a pair of socks. Outside the darkness of night was creeping on the brightness of evening. Walter wasn't home from the fair yet but she was expecting him. The fair finished on Sunday and if he had bought a couple of foals it would give him all he could do to reach the house before dark.

She was just finishing the last few stitches on top of the sock when she heard the sound of horses' hooves approaching the house. She jumped out of her chair and left the four knitting needles and the sock in the place where she was sitting. Out she went and opened the stable door so that her husband could guide the foals or horses he had bought into the stable without too much trouble. As soon as the three foals were tied up in the stable he took the saddle from the black horse and tied him in his own stall. After he had left a few sops of hay for the foals and put a handful of oats in a bowl under the horse's head, he hung the s addle on the crook behind the horse. Lucinda went back into the house without so much as greeting him.

She had caught hold of the sock and had her eyes fixed on her work by the time Sly came in the door. He looked in the direction of the fire beside which Lucinda was intent on her knitting.

'Are you thinking of boiling a pot of potatoes on that bonfire you have there?' he began. 'Upon my soul but you have two bags of turf burning in the heart of that fire.'

She looked hatefully in his direction.

'I haven't had a noggin of whiskey or a man to lie beside me for three nights,' she fumed.

'Ah, my good woman,' Sly placated her. 'Like everyone else I like a good fire, but if you had your way you'd burn all the turf in Ireland.'

Lucinda got up without another word, got a plate from the dresser and put the hot shoulder of mutton that was in an oven at the side of the fire on his plate. There were half a dozen potatoes in the oven as well and she put them on his plate also.

Sly sat at the table and ate the food hungrily. He left the plate as clean as if it had been licked by the dog.

'I suppose you had enough to drink at the weekend?' Lucinda reproached him.

Sly looked at her, none too pleased at what she had said.

'I hadn't,' he told her, 'but since you mention whiskey I'm going to saddle the horse again and go to town for a few.'

Oh boy! When Lucinda heard this she jumped to her feet.

'I have been here with three days and three nights,' she turned on him, 'milking, churning and baking while you have been roving all over the country drinking and throwing your arse about. You're only a few minutes inside the door of the house when you're thinking of getting on your horse to go drinking with your friends. Do you mind telling me where the money is coming from?'

Sly was not accustomed to having a woman barking questions at him.

'There was plenty of money in this house before you set your foot on the kitchen floor and, before you go any farther with this cross questioning, it's none of your business,' Sly replied.

When she heard this, Lucinda exploded.

'Upon my soul,' she shouted, 'if it's the money you got from Langstrom for my house and farm that you're throwing away, it is my business.'

That stopped Sly in his tracks. How did she find out when she was in the house for three days?

'Tell me who told you I sold your holding?' he demanded. 'And, to put matters right, from the day you were willing to marry me it was mine from then on.'

'But you promised to lease the house and the grazing of the land,' Lucinda replied crossly.

'I made every attempt to do that and I completely failed,' Sly told her. 'The holding was too small. I got a good price for the house and land together. Even Langstrom doesn't know what he'll do with it but I suppose he had too much dry cash in his house and it was safer to invest some of it in a patch of land.'

Lucinda shoved her face into Sly's.

'You stump of a fool,' she began. 'I'll bet he didn't tell you that he was willed the land next to mine by an uncle who died a month ago.'

'What would that have to do with the price of land?' Sly replied in a dour voice.

'Because it would add to his farm and he has a house on his land now which he hadn't until he bought my holding,' Lucinda told him.

Sly realised, on hearing this, that he had made a big mistake but couldn't find it in his heart to admit it. He took his cap that was hanging on the wall and hurried towards the door.

'I won't be long. As soon as I quench the thirst I got on the road I'll come home,' he promised her.

He opened the front door and Lucinda followed him.

'Off you go,' she said, 'and stay out till morning if it suits you but sleep in the stable when you come home because both doors will be barred.'

'Do that and you will find one of the bars in two halves in the middle of the kitchen and you will be on your way out to the stable,' Sly replied scathingly.

Lucinda slammed the door after him. She stood in the middle of the kitchen and began to cry.

'Oh, Lucinda Singleton,' she wailed, 'you didn't make a good bed for yourself at the end of your life.'

She sat by the fire looking to see if she would get an answer to her troubles in the flames. Would she bar the doors or would she let it pass on this occasion and go to bed? She got up and made to bolt the doors twice but changed her mind. She thought that, maybe with the whiskey in him, he would go out of his mind and injure her. For some time now, Walter Sly had been changing in his demeanour. He wasn't the same man that wooed her into marrying him. Maybe this was the real Walter Sly that was emerging. You have to live with someone to know them. He had sold her house without telling her. Where would she go if she had to escape from her husband? She was too old to begin afresh. 'Yes,' she conceded, 'I made my bed and now I'll have to lie in it and take the rough with the smooth.'

It was late that night before Lucinda lay under the covers. Her husband hadn't returned. She didn't sleep but was listening carefully, expecting every minute to hear the sound of the horse's hooves trotting down the boreen. She was tossing and turning for a long time with every sort of thought racing through her head. 'If he is drunk,' she thought, 'he will be looking for his conjugal rights and he will have no pity for me lying under him. It took me a few days to walk properly after he was astride me the last time. Upon my soul, he's only an animal.'

Despite her best efforts, she fell asleep. She woke with a fright with her husband pulling her from the bed on to the floor.

'Are you the strap who was going to bar the doors of my house?' he bellowed. He was blind drunk.

'In God's name, Walter,' she pleaded, 'have you lost your mind?'

He lifted her off the ground. She was screaming like a baby.

'After I shared my house with you, you strap,' he continued, 'you should respect me under my own roof.'

Then he stripped the clothes from her back and kicked her in her belly so hard that she fell against the wall. He went into the kitchen, got the horse whip and beat her unmercifully, then took her clothes and threw them down on her.

'Go out yourself and sleep in the loft of the stable,' he roared. 'Isn't that the bed you were giving me when I came home this evening?'

Lucinda attempted to get to her feet while all the time Sly was whipping her. Then he caught her by the hair. He pulled her to the kitchen and then in the direction of the front door. He gave her three more lashes of the whip and threw her out the door. He slammed the door after her.

Lucinda heard him bar the door inside. She realised then that she would have to sleep in the loft of the stable. She ran across the haggard crying so loudly that she could be heard far from home.

'Oh,' she cried, 'hadn't I a fine life before I saw Oldleighlin. It would have been easy to see that if the old man I married was in any way eligible he'd have been picked up years ago, but that didn't happen until Lucinda Singleton, the fool, came along. My God, it isn't good to be too gullible in this life.'

She went in the stable door. It was pitch black. The three foals began to jump in the air when they heard the crying and talking near them. She stopped crying and shouting and began to feel her way in the dark.

After a while, she laid her hand on the ladder that led to the loft. As soon as she was safely up in the loft she put on the clothes Sly had stripped off her. She was glad she had her clothes as there was a chill in the air from the frost outside and the north wind was whistling through the stable's old window. The loft was half full of hay which could easily be let down into the horses' manger during the winter. When Lucinda had put on her clothes, she made a nest for herself in the hay and covered her body with it too. After a long time, during which she was considering her plight, she fell into a deep sleep and, unusually for her, she had a terrible nightmare.

In it, her husband, Walter Sly, was above her; she was tied to a tree; Sly had two hooves like a donkey's and he had a four-pronged pike with which he was attempting to stab her. Beside the tree there was a big, deep hole and there was a blazing fire at the bottom. There were people in the middle of the fire pleading for mercy from anyone who would put out the fire . . .

Lucinda woke in a cold sweat. The second time she woke she couldn't close her eyes again so afraid was she. No woman was ever as grateful as Lucinda when morning dawned. She knew that she wouldn't be able to suffer many nights like the one before she went out of her mind. But she didn't know where to go or who to turn to. Her heart missed a beat when the stable door opened. Walter was at the door. He stood peering up at the loft.

'Lucinda,' he said, 'come into the house and make breakfast for me and have a bite yourself. Then go about your jobs and we'll forget about what happened last night.'

That took her by surprise. Yes, that would do until she thought of a better plan. At least she would have the comfort of the house. She had her own churn and could earn a few shillings herself. But surely there was something she could do with the animal she had married.

Lucinda stayed in the loft until Sly left the door. She climbed down with one eye on the door and the other on the rungs of the ladder. As she crossed the haggard she saw her husband going up through the field with some jute bags under his oxter. 'Thanks be to God,' she said to herself. Sly had put down the fire. What is seldom is wonderful. She took the skillet and hung it on the crook in order to boil the porridge. She put four eggs into the kettle that was singing on the side of the hearth. Breakfast was just ready when Sly came in the door.

'I could eat a horse,' Sly began as if nothing had happened the previous night. But Lucinda had learned a hard lesson. From now on, she would be very careful with every word she spoke in front of her animal of a husband.

In the weeks and months after that night, Sly drank less. He concentrated on the work of the farm but, then, in the middle of February, the cows began to calve and, as soon as a calf was three weeks old, Sly would take it to the fair. He began drinking again and very often Lucinda wouldn't see him until she had the cows milked in the morning.

One morning while they were eating breakfast, Lucinda felt that Sly was in good humour.

'Walter,' she began, 'do you remember at the start of the winter we were saying that, maybe, when things got busy on the farm, you would hire a servant girl or boy? More than half the herd are milking and all the work is falling to me this past fortnight. Before long, I'll be churning twice a week.'

Sly didn't reply for a few seconds.

'Look, Lucinda,' he answered eventually, 'leave it with me for a few days.'

Sly had to go to the fair a few days afterwards as he was selling three of his calves, from three weeks to a month old. It so happened that calves of that age were in great demand with cattle buyers from north Munster. Some of the big farmers did no churning. They concentrated on dry stock for the British market. They had large holdings with fertile land that could grow plenty of grass and wheat at little cost. Sly kept some of the heifer calves as his cows were getting old and he liked to keep his own breed of cattle. As well as that, he had more than enough milk left after churning with two-year-old cattle turning their noses up at it.

Tuesday was the day of the fair for young calves in Carlow. Sly got up early that morning, put the turf rail on the cart with a sop of straw in the bottom and harnessed the black horse to the cart. It was a hard, cold March morning with an icy edge to it. Farmers used to be afraid that the cold weather would give their calves the scour and the only remedy they had for it was to mix a fistful of flour in hot water containing four spoonfuls of glucose.

There were a few hundred calves for sale at the fair that day and it didn't take Sly long to sell his three animals. That was no wonder as they were fed on new milk from the day they were born. Some farmers would take the cream from the top of the milk for churning and feed the buttermilk to their calves. There would be a gloss on the calves fed on new milk that the other calves wouldn't have.

As soon as Sly had sold his calves and the money was in his

pouch, he headed straight for Langstrom's as he usually did. There were a dozen farmers there before him, all of whom had sold their calves.

When he had got a glass of whiskey from Langstrom and had saluted some of the farmers he knew, he found a seat near the bottom of the counter and sat down contentedly without talking to anybody. He was pondering how he could satisfy the strap of a woman he was married to.

'She is a top-class worker,' he conceded, 'but when something gets into her head, I make out that the seventeen devils from hell get into her to put her astray.'

When every customer had a drink in his hand, Langstrom went over in Sly's direction; he wanted to find out if he had cooled down since the time he bought his wife's holding from him without telling him that it was beside the farm he had been willed by his uncle.

'Has the last cow calved for you, Walter?' he enquired delicately.

'No,' Sly replied, 'not until the end of April. Christ, I'm crippled from work with a while. That strap I married has my heart broken. I had to let her know that I wear the trousers in my own house. But there were times when she was getting stubborn and trying to put the trousers on herself. That said, she is a great worker and, with the extra work I have to do with the cattle I have added to my herd, I can't do all the farm work. When all the cows have calved, I'll take someone in service. You don't, by any chance, know any strong young girl who is scratching her backside for lack of work?'

Langstrom looked at him, surprised.

'My good man,' he smiled, 'any young girl who has any appearance is in service in one of the big houses working in the kitchen by day and rattling the boards of the bed with the landlords by night. But, if it is a servant boy you want, there is a strapping young man at the top of the counter who is ready to go in service to any farmer who will hire him for a season.'

Sly looked at the young man and examined him from head to toe. He was strongly built and had a civil appearance.

'Send him down to me in a while,' Sly instructed Langstrom, 'but don't let on that we were talking about him. Upon my soul, but they are constantly looking for more and more money from season to season. I'll pretend that I might be hiring a man, and then again, that I might not.'

Langstrom went about this business. While Sly was drinking another glass of whiskey, he noticed Langstrom's head inclining in the direction of the young man. He took the drink that was in front of him and began walking towards Sly. He stopped at the empty space in the counter near Sly. He put his drink on the counter and looked cautiously over and back.

'I'm told you're looking to hire a farm worker,' he said steadily.

'Maybe I am and maybe I am not,' Sly replied nonchalantly.

'I won't ask you again,' the young man countered, 'because I have almost made up my mind to go to the fertile plain of Munster. I have seen nothing since I came to this county but small farmers with petty, narrow minds and they are as miserly as Midas.'

That knocked a start out of Sly.

'Take it nice and easy,' he advised him. 'Maybe you have met only the worst of us. And, yes, I am looking for a farm worker. Could you stay until the beginning of May?'

'I wouldn't,' the young man told him. 'Live horse and you'll get grass is your plan, is it?'

'Oh, not at all,' Sly assured him. 'What would you say to a year's hire instead of a season's hire, starting next Monday?'

The young man dropped his drink on the counter when he heard that.

'That is, if your work is satisfactory,' Sly added.

He wouldn't throw his money away. He was too old for that.

'I am a good milker, a good workman,' the young man informed him. 'I can plough a field with a team of horses with a light or heavy scribe, whichever suits the land. I am told that you buy and sell foals and horses. There is no man within fifty miles of here who can break a young colt as well as I can. I can churn as well as any woman and can bake bread as well. Have you any other questions?'

'The Devil a one,' Sly retorted, 'but that it is a pity I didn't meet you before I married my wife.'

They both laughed out loud.

'I'll pay you four pounds every three months and you will have a bed in the back kitchen and three meals a day beginning next Monday,' Sly informed him.

'I am Walter Sly,' he introduced himself, 'and my farm is in Oldleighlin.'

'People call me John Dempsey,' was the reply.

They had a few drinks together in order to get to know each other before they went their separate ways.

# Chapter Nine

Early the following Monday morning the sun was shining on the green fields of Bilboa and up as far as the town of Oldleighlin. Lucinda Sly was driving in the cows for milking. Walter Sly was still snoring, his head hanging out of the bed on account of his drinking the previous night. Lucinda had a habit of talking out loud to herself if anything was bothering her, which was often since she married Sly.

What she was saying to herself this morning was that her patience was exhausted with regard to Sly's drinking, not to mention that every bone in her body was aching from the beating she got from Sly and all the work she had to do on the farm. The day would come when she would stab him in the belly with the four-pronged pike while he was sleeping in bed.

She didn't see the man who was walking down the boreen behind her and could hear every word she said. He followed her to the cowshed without interrupting her. When she had guided the last cow into the shed she saw him and screamed loudly with the start she got.

'Easy, woman,' the man said. 'I'm the farm worker your husband hired. Didn't he tell you about me?'

She spent a while staring at him as if he had two heads.

'A farm worker,' she gasped. 'He didn't say a word to me about it. But, thanks be to God, it's not before time. I'm Lucinda Sly. The Oldleighlin drunkard is still snoring. Listen, I have a habit of thinking out loud. Did you hear what I said?'

'I didn't catch a word you said,' he lied. 'I was too far away from you. By the way, I'm John Dempsey. If you like, I'll milk the cows with you.'

Lucinda's heart lifted when she heard this.

'Oh, God be with you forever,' she exclaimed. 'It was He sent you to me. I am dying with pains in my bones since the start of last winter.'

They began milking. When a cow was milked, the pail of milk was strained into a big wooden tub. Little by little Lucinda would glance at the fine man the morning had brought her. A talkative man, a pleasant man, she reasoned, and a man who could get milk from the toughest cow.

They were stripping the last two cows when Walter Sly stuck his head in the door of the shed. He got a start when he saw Dempsey.

'My soul to the devil,' he blurted, 'you are here already.'

'He is here,' Lucinda answered, 'and he has milked the cows with me. Oh, boy! A noted milker. Will you go in, Walter, and hang the skillet of porridge over the fire?'

'God be with you, woman,' Dempsey spoke. 'My belly is tied to my backbone with the hunger.'

Sly went towards the house without saying a word.

'Look at that for blackguarding,' Lucinda said to Dempsey. 'If you weren't here I would have got a belt of the cows' spancel across the side of the head.'

'Why would he do such a thing?' Dempsey was surprised.

'Because I told him to hang the skillet over the fire,' Lucinda said.

When he heard this, Dempsey didn't say a word but strained the pail of milk into the tub.

'Have you any special place where you wash the pails?' Dempsey asked her.

'Turn yours upside down outside the door,' she told him. 'I'll wash it myself when I have seen to the calves.'

Sly spent a week showing Dempsey what was to be done on the farm. Dempsey found out that he wouldn't be idle while he was in service with Walter Sly. But, that said, Sly was married to a friendly woman who was an excellent cook. When it was drawing near suppertime, he would get the fine smell of baking coming through the kitchen door. Oh, it would give an appetite to one who had none.

As soon as Sly considered that his hired hand was familiar with the farm work, he let him know that he wouldn't be around the farm as often during the day in the coming months as he would be buying and selling horses. He had shown him how to run the farm and Dempsey would have to do the work. If there was ploughing or digging to be done, he would have to do it. If Lucinda needed a hand around the sheds or with the churning, he would have to help her, not to mention doing the spring sowing and the autumn harvesting as well. Dempsey's heart lifted on hearing this as Sly was an awkward man at the best of times, and when he had a few drinks in him, he was worse. There was no need for Sly to show Dempsey how to run the farm because as soon as Sly had left him, Dempsey did the work his own way.

John Dempsey's bed was in the back kitchen, which had a door leading out to the back haggard and the sheds. He could go out if he needed to make his water in the middle of the night and there was plenty of room beside the ditch for that. If a pin dropped in any room by day or by night, Dempsey could hear it as there was no door between the kitchen and Lucinda and Walter's room, only a curtain so that they would have privacy. Dempsey would cover his ears when Sly came home having been gone, very often, from early morning until dawn the following day. No need to mention that his belly would be full of drink. It was Lucinda, the poor creature, who got the short end of the stick. Many times Dempsey had to restrain himself from going into their room and giving Sly a drubbing.

A season went by and Dempsey saw little of Sly by day. He had sown two acres of potatoes along with a couple of acres of oats, not to mention a half acre of turnips and the same of mangolds. Ben Stacey, Sly's nearest neighbour, spent a week ploughing with Dempsey and Dempsey returned the favour when Stacey was doing the spring sowing. Neither of them wanted Sly with them as he wasn't the neatest of workers when it came to sowing, but give him a colt to break and he would be in his element.

When he wasn't at a fair, Sly spent most of his days drinking in Langstrom's and fighting with the buyers he used to deal with.

One day he was fighting with the Brennans, who used to live close by his own farm but who he had evicted a year earlier. One of the Brennans threatened to kill him. There were three of them and they were strong men.

When he got home, Lucinda put his supper before him. He was in a foul humour and had a couple of deep cuts on his cheek and on his eyebrow. He got up out of his chair by the fire and he almost stumbled as he was pulling it towards the table.

'Where was the fair today?' Lucinda asked sarcastically. 'In Langstrom's tavern I suppose.'

John Dempsey was just coming in the door. He saw the mood Sly was in and looked fearfully at Lucinda, who was taking a joint of mutton from a skillet that she had put on the side of the fire. Although Sly had had a lot to drink, he saw his opportunity for a treacherous attack on her. He got up drunkenly from his chair. Lucinda was bent over taking the mutton from the skillet when Sly drew a kick on her and she banged her head against the leg of the hob. When Dempsey saw that, he could turn a blind eye no longer. He punched Sly so hard in the face that he collapsed on the flat of his back in the middle of the kitchen.

'Come on now, you bastard,' he exploded. 'What kind of a man would kick a woman?'

Lucinda got up gingerly, looked fondly at Dempsey and then turned to look at her husband stretched groaning on the kitchen floor.

'I hope the bastard is dead,' she spat.

She put her arms around Dempsey's waist and kissed him.

'How did a kind, pleasant woman like you marry that animal?' he began. 'Leave this house or you will go out the front door in a white deal box. You are married to a madman.'

Lucinda kissed Dempsey again. That put a different complexion on things but Dempsey put such thoughts out of his head. He picked Sly off the ground and tossed him into the chair.

Although he was only half Lucinda's age, Dempsey had the same feelings for her that he would have had for a younger woman. Sly was still not stirring in the chair but soon they heard him snoring intermittently. They knew then that he was in a drunken sleep and he wouldn't wake up even if the house fell on him. Lucinda caught Dempsey by the hand and guided him to the bedroom.

This didn't surprise him as, from the way she looked at him this past while, he knew that she desired him and that Sly was giving her no satisfaction in bed. Dempsey was a confirmed bachelor and it had been a long time since he had lain with a woman. He knew that Lucinda was a good woman who wouldn't betray a secret.

Sly didn't wake up until dawn. He had no memory of the blow in the face he got from Dempsey, or, if he had, he didn't pretend to, but that was the first night Lucinda and John Dempsey lay together and it was the beginning of their troubles.

Every day, as soon as Sly left home, Dempsey would hurry

through the fields towards the house and it wasn't always to have a bite to eat. He would help Lucinda with the churning and milking as well. But he wasn't always able to save her from Sly's fists. He advised Lucinda to go for advice to the minister of her church unknown to Sly for fear she would get a worse beating from him.

One day as she was returning home from the butter market in Carlow it happened that she was passing the minister's house. She halted her horse and cart outside his gate. She tied the horse's reins to the poll and faced the door. Her heart was throbbing. How could she tell a stranger that her husband was constantly abusing her? She knocked on the door. It opened suddenly. The minister, John Doyne, was at the door.

'Oh Lucinda,' he greeted her. 'Come in, come in! What brings you here? Look, sit on the chair. The maid will bring you some food.'

'There's no need,' Lucinda responded. 'I'm on my way home from the market and I will have to milk the cows and do other jobs when I get there. I have come for your help and advice. My husband beats me unmercifully when he comes home from the tavern at night full of whiskey.'

The minister looked at her in surprise.

'Are you telling me,' he asked in disbelief, 'that Walter Sly beats his wife? I have known that man for years and he wouldn't hurt a fly.'

'I'm telling you,' she repeated, 'that if somebody doesn't talk to him, my body will be buried in the cemetery before long.'

On hearing this, the minister jumped from his chair.

'Go home, my good woman,' he said, 'and do your duty as a wife. Prepare his food, patch his clothes and do your duty in the marriage bed and don't let me see you at my door with balls of lies coming out of your mouth. Off you go now. Soon women will be looking for the vote or a seat in parliament. The cheek of them.'

Poor Lucinda went out the door more confused than she was going in. When she reached home, Dempsey was driving in the cattle. She enquired had he seen any sight of her husband.

'I don't think he'll be at home until late tonight,' Dempsey replied. 'He took the white colt. He said he had twenty miles of road before him.'

Lucinda's heart lit up when she heard this. Dempsey unyoked the horse and led it into the field before helping Lucinda with the milking.

While they were milking, Lucinda told him about her visit to the minister. She was so upset that she had to lay her head against the cow's belly for a rest before she could continue milking.

'Oh, John,' she pleaded, 'what am I to do now? I am denied by my own Church. "Go home", the minister told me, "and do your duty as a good wife" and he mentioned the bed too . . . As if he could do anything in bed. He is too heavy with drink, it takes him ten minutes to locate it and when he does he has nothing but a bit of wrinkled skin. I can see that he is spreading rumours about me around the place. Hardly any of the women who sell butter on the side of the street salute me now. Yes, and those who do, call me "the hag of the butter".'

'Ah, my good woman,' Dempsey soothed her, 'they are jealous

of you because of the quality of your butter.'

When the milk had been poured from the tub into the dishes in the dairy, they both washed the pails and headed for the house.

Dempsey had put down a big turf fire as he knew, with Sly gone and not due to return until late that night, they would have a fine cosy time by the fire. That was the night that Lucinda put the thought in Dempsey's mind that there was room in her bed for only one man and that he, Dempsey, was her choice.

On hearing this, Dempsey grew afraid. He was happy enough with the way things were between Lucinda and himself. Never in his life had he got so much pleasure from a woman as he had from this gentle woman. But the battering she received from her husband when he, Dempsey, wasn't around to protect her greatly disturbed him. 'Right so,' Dempsey thought to himself, 'what is the solution to the problem? He is often enough seated on the chair where I am sitting.'

'What can we do about Walter?' he suddenly blurted out loud.

'Look at the axe by the wall of the house,' Lucinda pointed out. 'One blow with the edge of that axe will split his head.'

Dempsey sat back on the chair with two wide eyes.

'That's murder,' he protested. 'Do you know what happens to murderers? They are hanged.'

'You are right, John,' she persisted. 'If there is any proof against the one who did the deed. You could stay here as a farm hand and we could bar the two doors of the house every night and what do you think would happen?'

'I know you are at the end of your tether with Walter,' Dempsey continued, 'but murder! In God's name, gather your senses, Lucinda. I never heard of anybody who did such a deed escaping the gallows.'

'What kind of man are you at all?' Lucinda taunted him. 'Or have you any feelings for me?'

This struck him like a blow to his face.

'Look, Lucinda,' he went on, 'leave it to me. We'll have to come up with a better plan than splitting his head with an axe. Think of all the blood that would be around the kitchen.'

Lucinda's face lit up on hearing this as she felt that Dempsey was a clever man who would come up with a better way of getting rid of Sly. She got out of her chair and sat on his knee. They spent some time fondling each other.

'We had better go to bed before Walter returns,' Dempsey urged her.

Up they went to the bedroom and such was Dempsey's desire for Lucinda that he was ripping the buttons of his flap on the way.

They were only a minute in the bed when they heard the latch of the door being lifted. They looked at each other.

'Did you bar both doors?' Lucinda asked him, afraid that her husband had returned.

They jumped out of the bed, both searching for their own clothes. Who was standing at the room door but Bridget Massey, a friend of the Slys. She stood there goggle-eyed looking at the two naked figures before her, Dempsey looking for his trousers and Lucinda trying to cover her body.

'Oh God protect us,' Bridget wailed, 'but the Devil's work is going on in this house of damnation this evening.'

'I know what you think we are doing,' Lucinda began, 'but the opposite is the case. The bed is full of fleas. John was trying to get rid of them when they got into our clothes.'

Bridget turned and went straight for the door.

'Upon my soul,' she exclaimed, 'I have seen people beating a blanket with a bat but I never saw two naked people killing fleas without one.'

She went out the door taking out her rosary beads for the house and its inhabitants . . . that God would be merciful and forgive their sins and that he would banish Lucifer to the hobs of hell.

'What will we do now?' Dempsey asked. 'If she opens her mouth you will be as good as dead, Lucinda.'

Lucinda thought a moment.

'Leave it to me,' she reassured him. 'I will visit her tomorrow and I will bring her a lump of butter and a dozen eggs. She knows well what kind of man Walter Sly is.'

'Tell me if you think she is loose with the tongue,' Dempsey pleaded.

'Look,' Lucinda informed him, 'even if she is, she is of the breed of the tinkers. Sure, nobody believes a word they say even if it was in the confession box.'

By the time Sly reached home that night, or the following morning I should say, it wasn't far from cockcrow. Nearly the whole village heard him with his shouting and bawling like a madman. Dempsey was in his own bed in the back kitchen and

Lucinda had one eye open in her own bed. She heard the front door opening and then the thud of Sly's drunken body falling into the middle of the kitchen.

'Lucinda,' he demanded, 'get up and get me some food.'

Lucinda pretended not to hear him. Sly went down to the bedroom, caught her by the hair of the head, pulled her out on to the floor and down to the kitchen. Then he began to kick her.

'All right,' she shouted in fear, 'give me a chance to wake up.'

Just then Dempsey came into the room from the back kitchen in his drawers. When he saw the abuse Sly was meting out to his wife, he jumped in between them. He told Lucinda to sit down on the chair.

'But I have to prepare food for Walter,' she whimpered fearfully.

'By the time I'm finished with him, he won't have much mind for food,' Dempsey promised her catching the collar of Sly's coat and letting fly with his left fist to Sly's jaw. He punched Sly with his right and left until he was on the flat of his back. He lifted him from the ground then and took him to the bed.

'Now, my good woman,' Dempsey addressed Lucinda, 'he has no need for food or to put you to the trouble of preparing it.'

Lucinda burst out laughing.

'That's the first time I've heard you laughing in three months,' Dempsey smiled. 'You should laugh more often.'

'Oh, John,' Lucinda replied, 'you should have stayed out of this mess. When he wakes up in the morning he'll give you the road.'

'Indeed he won't,' Dempsey assured her. 'Don't you remember

the last time I gave him a couple of thumps; he blamed his neighbour, Michael Connors. Off to sleep with you now and don't be in any way worried.'

# Chapter Ten

Midsummer, 1834. Walter Sly had added extra cows to his herd. A person not in the know would say that he had added to his herd to improve his farm but that was not so; he did it to add to Lucinda's and Dempsey's workload so that they would be so exhausted in the evening that they would have no time for romance.

Michael Connors, Sly's neighbour, had whispered in his ear that Lucinda and Dempsey were becoming very fond of each other . . . Yes, and that it was no wonder that he was getting pleasure where Sly once was. Rumours were going around that Lucinda was the worst kind of witch. Even the women who sold butter beside her on the street in Carlow had turned against her because at that time there was no worse sin than a woman having an affair with a man who was not her husband. Some of the bigwigs' wives were engaged in such practices, it was said. Many of them were banished but it was seldom spoken about as they were sent on a long holiday never to return.

Lucinda spent a hard summer and autumn as more animals were out on pasture and extra fodder had to be provided for them for the winter. Walter Sly spent most of the summer going to fairs enjoying himself and drinking heavily. That was the summer that Lucinda was at her wits' end, and, but for John Dempsey's help and friendship, she would have been put into the lunatic asylum. Her bones were protruding through her skin, she had lost so much weight.

The November Fair was the one Walter Sly most looked forward to as it was held in Carlow town. He would always have two or three horses ready for it. It was a hard, dry Saturday morning with a frosty breeze that was blowing from the north as is usual in November. Lucinda and Dempsey milked the two cows that weren't dry yet. As soon as the three of them had eaten breakfast, Sly ordered Dempsey to inspect the boundary ditches and to make any necessary repairs. Dempsey went out the front door and over the ditch into the field. Sly watched him until he disappeared from sight. Lucinda knew that something was irritating him and that he didn't want Dempsey to be present.

No sooner was Dempsey out of sight than Sly turned on Lucinda and hit her across the face.

'For the last couple of months,' he snarled, 'the butter money is short. Is this how you are paying your stallion for his services?'

He hit her again and went to the bottom of the kitchen. He took the bowl from the top of the dresser and shoved his hand into it. He took out two pounds.

'What's this?' he bellowed. 'Or do you think you are married to a stump of a fool?'

Then he smashed the bowl on the floor. He put the money into a pouch that was already bulging with notes. Lucinda burst into tears.

'It was my mother who gave me that bowl for my first marriage,' she sobbed.

Sly caught another bowl and smashed it. Lucinda could bear this no longer. She went down to the dresser, took four mugs that were in the house before she married Sly and smashed them on the floor.

'Any fool, woman or man, can smash ware on the floor,' she cried, walking away from him.

At this, Sly's face turned the colour of a turnip.

'As soon as I get a chance,' he fumed, 'I'm going into the attorney to take your name off my will and, if there's any sight of you when I come home tonight, I'll make a skillet of your head.'

He rushed out to the stable, saddled his horse, put headstalls on the two young horses he was ready to sell at the fair, jumped on his horse's back and tightened the reins he had on the two horses.

'Go on,' he bellowed in a voice so harsh that the horses ran as fast as they could down the boreen.

It was hunger that reminded John Dempsey that it was time to head for the house. Lucinda had boiled a pig's head and a pot of potatoes. As soon as he came in the door, she got a fright.

'Oh, God save us,' she exclaimed, 'I thought it was Walter who was there.'

She turned her back to him as if she were concealing something.

'What's the big secret you are hiding from me at the table?' Dempsey enquired.

'You won't believe this,' Lucinda began, 'but before Walter left he lost his head with me. He hit me a few times with his fists and broke some of my delf on the floor. And he found the money I was hiding in the bowl. I have seen him mad many times but I have never seen white froth coming from his mouth until today. He said he would make a skillet of my head when he came home . . . Oh, John,' she sighed, 'I will be got dead in the morning.'

Dempsey saw a wooden box on the floor.

'What's in the box?' he asked Lucinda.

'When Walter was beating me,' she told him, 'I saw something falling on the floor. I thought at first that it was some sort of pin. I stayed where I was until he had gone for a while. I picked it up from the ground. What was there but a key. I hadn't the courage until now to find out what the key would open but it is suitable to open this box that was under the bed. You won't believe what is in the box.'

'Upon my soul,' Dempsey observed, 'from the state of your eye, it wasn't a slap you got but the fist.'

Then he walked to the side of the table.

'Oh my!' he exclaimed taking a gun from the box. 'I wonder which one of us he was going to kill with this . . . Yes, and it is ready for use.'

'What do you mean?' Lucinda asked him, trembling.

'What I mean is that there is a bullet in the gun. A person couldn't be more prepared than that.'

They looked at each other and then at the gun.

'But we have the gun now,' said Lucinda with fire in her eyes.

'Ah Lucinda,' Dempsey pleaded, 'didn't I tell you before to put those thoughts from your mind?'

She turned on him. 'John Dempsey,' she began, 'have you any backbone? Look! It's very simple. We will both stay up tonight until whatever time he comes home. He will be blind drunk as usual. When he is seated in the chair and fast asleep, then we will do the deed.'

Dempsey wasn't too happy with the plan but Lucinda explained to him that there were horse dealers who weren't too happy with Sly and were out to get him for a long time and that it was he, Sly, who circulated that story. They would both take Sly's body out to the haggard and she would go looking for the neighbours' help.

'What will we do with the gun?' Dempsey interjected.

'We will put it in the box and back where we found it,' Lucinda told him animatedly.

'This is our last chance to get rid of suffering and a bad marriage at the same time. Aren't we the two who would work this farm together,' she coaxed him.

'It's as well for us to have a bite of food first before I lose my appetite,' Dempsey replied.

When she heard this, Lucinda knew that she had a partner who would do the deed with her.

The horse fair in Carlow town was on 8 November 1834, and it was the biggest horse fair in the county. Buyers and men selling horses came from all over Ireland. Walter Sly knew most of them well from travelling from fair to fair. The horse buyers were big spenders and big drinkers and they knew their business.

It is said that the day you buy an animal is the day you sell it. Let me explain – if you buy a good animal, you will be able to sell it later on even if the price is high. The November fair in Carlow was the one where every breed and kind of horse was for sale from the work horse to the hunter, not to mention cobs, mules, jennets and donkeys. Everyone, from the highest gentlemen to the tinkers of the road, was at the fair and if a particular buyer didn't know enough about buying an animal, an unscrupulous one would quickly fool him up to his eyes.

Walter Sly tied the two horses he had for sale to a ring outside Langstrom's. He stabled the horse that would bring him home in Langstrom's stable and put an armful of hay under his head.

Frances Campbell had a couple of horses for sale too. She was the wife of a man who held a seat in the House of Lords in England. They had stables in counties Carlow and Kildare. Before he married, Sly often had a drink with Frances and they would go home together when her husband was away in the House of Lords. Nothing much was made of it as they went home the same road or most of it anyway. But it used be said that Sly went the extra mile to her house with her for fear she would be attacked by tinkers. Some of Langstrom's customers remembered her advising Sly against marrying Lucinda Singleton some years previously.

Frances was standing beside the two horses she had for sale as Sly was coming back from the stable. 'Let's go into the tavern,

Frances,' Sly invited her, 'and we'll wash down the dust of the road.'

Frances only wanted the word. They both went in. They went into the card room at the back of the bar because women weren't allowed to drink in the main bar at that time. They drank each other's, and the King's, health.

'I haven't seen much of you this past while,' Sly began.

'I spend most of the year in London now that my husband has been promoted in the House of Lords and, since he got his new post, my heart is broken,' Frances said with disdain.

Sly looked at her.

'Is it how you don't like the city life?' he asked her.

Frances shook herself.

'I hate that city,' she volunteered.

'And what takes you over there so?' Sly persisted.

'Because it came to my ears that he was getting fond of a floosie who works as his secretary,' she informed him.

When he heard this, Sly burst out laughing.

'Isn't he entitled to satisfy his desires?' he laughed. 'It's only human nature – and look who's talking! You're no angel yourself.'

Frances smiled when she heard this.

'It wasn't that he was playing around with his secretary that bothered me,' she confided in him, 'but when he wasn't eating supper at home, I was worried that he would give me the road. That is very common in England at the moment. Then how would I be, without a title or a shilling in my pouch? I'd be like a tinker's wife. But it's not that but this. How are you getting on since you got married?'

Sly shook himself and looked around the room in case anybody but Frances could hear him.

'You gave me good advice,' he complained, 'and I didn't take it. I thought I was marrying an angel of a woman. Oh! She is far from an angel. An out and out bitch. I'd be as well off with an oak plank beside me in bed. She is cold, quarrelsome, headstrong and she thinks she is wearing the trousers. Upon my soul, it would take me the rest of my life to explain.'

Frances and Sly didn't leave Langstrom's until the afternoon.

'Right,' said Sly stretching himself, 'if we don't go about our business, we will have to take our animals back home again.'

Out they went.

It was late in the evening when Sly sold his two yearlings to a buyer from a stable in Kildare. He headed for the tavern along with the buyer. That is where he would be paid for his horses and he would give the buyer a small sum for luck. He met other buyers he knew. Without a doubt he would have to take a few drinks in their company. It was the tradition at the fairs.

It was some time later when Frances Campbell came in. She had to spend more time out in the street before a buyer approached her. Ned Radwell, a neighbour of Sly's, joined them. Sly was very drunk but Frances wasn't quite as bad. It was about five o'clock and already it was dark outside.

Frances was the one with the most sense at the end of the evening.

'Walter,' she said, 'don't you think it is time to be going home?'

The three of them left when they had finished their drinks.

They went out to the stable and harnessed their horses for the road home. They took the road out by Graiguecullen and up towards Bilboa. When they reached Bilboa the three of them stopped for a last drink before they parted. They had a drink with Thomas Singleton, Lucinda's son who was in charge of the police station there. After a short time Frances and Ned left for home. Sly had only two more drinks with Singleton but, during that time, he let him know that Lucinda was becoming very cantankerous. Singleton told him that she used to be like that when he was young and that it would be better for Sly to take no notice of her. Singleton observed that Sly was blind drunk.

'Maybe I should harness my horse and go as far as your house with you,' he suggested when he saw that Sly was intent on going home.

'Ah, I pity your poor head,' Sly spoke in a slurred voice. 'Put me in my saddle and the horse will go to the house himself.'

Singleton kept his eye on Walter on the horse's back as they went off in the direction of Oldleighlin until they disappeared from sight at the turn of the road.

Lucinda was seated on a chair with John Dempsey opposite her on the other side of the fire and they had piled on extra turf as they weren't expecting Sly home until midnight. They were both nervous as they weren't sure that their plan was without fault but, as Lucinda said, it would be better to be in prison than to live the life she had with her blackguard of a husband. For a while Dempsey would be willing and, half an hour later, he would be in favour of abandoning the plan. But when Lucinda told him that she would take the full blame if things went wrong, he relaxed. He was a reasonably young man with his whole life before him. He was very fond of Lucinda but there is a great difference between being fond of somebody and being in love.

They had no lamp lit and they were depending on the fire to cast sufficient light around the kitchen. Lucinda told Dempsey that if Walter saw a light in the kitchen late at night he would become suspicious as she usually went to bed at nine o'clock during the winter. At twenty past ten they heard the sound of a horse's hooves coming down the boreen. They both jumped out of their chairs.

'You know what you have to do,' Lucinda spoke with a tremor in her voice. 'Go into the back kitchen and I'll go into the bedroom. Give him twenty minutes after he sits down in his chair. He should be sound asleep by then. Put your head out the door and if he is asleep come to the room door and you know the rest.'

From the humming they could both hear, they knew that Sly had drunk more than his fill. He always returned from the tavern humming and talking to himself.

The horse stopped in front of the stable. He tried twice to dismount but he nearly fell to the ground.

'I'll knock him off the horse,' Dempsey suggested to Lucinda.

'Do not,' she said, shivering with fear.

Sly succeeded in dismounting at the third attempt. They heard him coming in the door not without difficulty. Dempsey had a clear sight of him as he had left the door of the back kitchen ajar. In a short while Sly staggered into the chair. In a few short minutes he was snoring.

Lucinda and Dempsey went into the kitchen. Lucinda walked towards the axe that was standing against the wall. She gave it to Dempsey. He went up to Sly and raised it over his head but lowered it slowly towards the ground and moved back three steps.

'I can't do it,' he said in a low voice.

Lucinda took the axe from him and walked towards Sly but she couldn't do it either. Suddenly Dempsey found the courage and changed his mind. He took the axe from Lucinda's hand and landed a fierce blow on the side of Sly's head. He fell from his chair in a heap on the ground. Lucinda took the gun from her apron and gave it to Dempsey. Without hesitating he put a bullet in Sly's brain. They each caught Sly by an arm and dragged his body out into the haggard. Dempsey fired another bullet at the wall of the house. They would tell the police that the murderer fired that shot so that neither of them would come out until he had escaped. They both went into the house leaving Sly's body in the haggard. That is where it would be when the police arrived.

Neither of them slept that night but sat in front of the fire waiting for the eastern sky to brighten.

'I wonder if any of the neighbours heard the noise of the bullet when I fired that shot,' Dempsey said.

'We will soon know,' Lucinda answered looking at the axe with which he struck the fatal blow.

Dempsey got up out of his chair, took the axe, walked over to the fire and examined it in the light of the flames. He wanted to find out if there was any trace of blood on it. He got an old rag and wiped the axe with it. Then he put it back in its usual place.

'In the name of God, Lucinda,' he cried, 'what have we done? We will both be hanged surely.'

'We will if you open your big mouth,' Lucinda warned him. 'Shake yourself, man ... Wasn't it one of Walter's enemies who followed him home from the fair that shot him? I can tell you that Walter had a surplus of enemies in this parish not to mention throughout the county. About three years ago didn't he evict a family down the road – you know, the Brennans. Yes, and what about the horse buyers? Half of them are the breed of the Sheridans and of the tinkers. Some of those would kill you at the turn of a penny.'

That eased Dempsey somewhat.

'Yes,' he agreed. 'You are right without a doubt. Did you put the gun back into its box?'

'I didn't yet,' she admitted. 'I'll get the box. There's a half dozen bullets at the back. Put two of them into the gun and I'll put it back under the bed in our room.'

'I know nothing about guns,' Dempsey said, opening the back of the gun while Lucinda gave him two bullets.

He put them into the chamber, eased the hammer back and replaced it in the box.

They put no more turf on the fire – maybe there would be questions to be asked if a big fire was lighting when Lucinda called the neighbours. She put a couple of potatoes roasting in the embers and she asked Dempsey if he would eat a few. But he had no appetite after what he had done.

They spent the night sitting there looking across at each other and neither of them had much to say. Every minute was like an hour and every hour was like a week until at last the eastern sky began to brighten over the land.

'We will let day dawn and then I'll go for help. You stay with the body,' Lucinda said.

They waited another hour and by that time it was bright enough for Lucinda to take the short-cut through the field to her nearest neighbours.

She began to cry and shout when she was within fifty yards of Ben Stacey's front door. As soon as she got to his house she began to beat the door like a madwoman.

'Walter is dead! Walter is dead!' she shrieked. 'Get up, Ben, and help us!'

The door opened and there stood Ben in his drawers.

'In the name of God, woman, what's up with you?' he demanded.

'Somebody murdered my husband last night,' Lucinda wailed.

'Wait a few minutes,' Stacey replied, calming her. 'Draw your breath and tell me the whole story.'

'I was sitting by the fire late last night,' Lucinda sobbed, 'and waiting for Walter to come home from the fair. Dempsey had gone to sleep. I heard the horse trotting down the road. He stopped outside the stable door. I was just about to get up off my chair to put some food on the table for him. Then I heard another horse running at speed down the road and into the haggard. I heard a sound like the sound of a gun. I had reached the door by this time. I saw Walter falling from his horse. The rider of the other horse fired another bullet in the direction of the house and told me to go indoors and not to move until morning or he would put a bullet through my head as well. I ran into the kitchen. Dempsey had just gotten up and was standing beside me. I told him there was a madman on horseback outside in the haggard and that he had murdered Walter. He threatened that he would shoot anybody who put their head outside the door until morning. Go to the house – John Dempsey is there and I will go to the other neighbours for help.'

'Do not,' Stacey replied in panic. 'Go home and we will be with you without delay.'

Ben Stacey woke up the rest of the neighbours and, when he had done that, he went straight across the field to Walter Sly's house. When he reached the fateful place he saw Lucinda standing at the stable door staring at Walter's body. Dempsey was taking the saddle from Sly's horse and he released the animal out into the field near the house.

'Would you go to his body, Ben,' she begged him, 'and see if there is any spark of life in him. There should be a fistful of notes in one of his pockets and a pocket watch and chain in his waistcoat pocket.'

'I won't for a few minutes,' he replied with caution. 'The neighbours are coming. I'll wait for somebody to be beside me when I go through his pockets.'

John Griffin was the next neighbour to arrive. Stacey asked him to go to the body with him so that they could go through Sly's pockets. They searched his waistcoat pocket first looking for the watch, but not even the chain was there. They went through the rest of his pockets but they found nothing. No doubt it would have been difficult for them as Lucinda had ordered Dempsey to go through his pockets and she gave him the watch, as if it were a present, before she went to look for her neighbours' help. Lucinda told them it appeared that someone had followed him from the fair.

'Maybe,' she suggested, 'it was somebody who saw him getting money from a buyer as payment for the two horses he sold.'

It was a good, believable story to put before the police and the judge.

Lucinda asked Ben Stacey to go to the barracks in Bilboa to report the tragedy to the police and request that they come without delay. She said it would not be right to move the body from the place where the murder happened.

Lucinda expected that maybe it would be her son, Thomas Singleton, who would come as it was his mother's husband who had been murdered but he went to higher authority. Captain Battersby told him not to go near the house or the body until he himself was with him, and, even then, not to have anything to do with the case because of his relationship with the family. Because it was Sunday, it was some time after lunch when the police arrived at the scene. Captain Battersby and Thomas Singleton were the first to arrive along with a constable named Ernest Hudson. Thomas ran to his mother and hugged her. She told him the story that she and Dempsey had made up.

'Ah, Mam,' he advised her, 'you will have to tell your story to one of the other constables. I can't have hand, act or part in the case.'

Captain Battersby and Ernest Hudson examined the place where Sly's body lay and they examined the body as well even though the doctor was due later to perform a post-mortem.

Minister John Doyne arrived and he sympathised with Lucinda and the neighbours, most of whom were at the scene by now and each one had their own opinion about what had happened. Captain Battersby and Constable Ernest Hudson spent more than an hour examining the scene of the crime.

When the doctor arrived and had examined the body he spoke to the captain.

'It would appear,' he informed him, 'that the person who murdered this man was no more than a yard from him. His moustache is singed by the gunpowder.'

The captain approached Constable Hudson. 'What did his wife tell you,' he questioned him, 'that a horseman murdered him?'

'Yes, sir,' the policeman answered.

The captain looked at Lucinda and walked towards her. As soon as he drew near her, she took a few steps back and stood near Dempsey.

'You reported,' he began, 'that a horseman came into the haggard and fired a shot from a gun. How far from your husband was he when he fired that shot?'

Lucinda took a few seconds before she answered as she knew well that the captain had a reason for asking a question like that.

'Oh,' she replied, 'I suppose he was nine or ten yards from him.'

The captain looked at Lucinda suspiciously.

'Did your husband ever have a gun?' he continued.

'Oh, ah . . . I don't know,' she replied somewhat apprehensively.

Her son was present when she made that answer.

He looked directly at the captain.

'He had a handgun he got a few years ago when he evicted the Brennans,' he informed him. 'They swore he would be found dead in a ditch.'

'There was no gun by the body when I asked Ben Stacey and John Griffin to search his pockets,' Lucinda offered. 'He sold a pair of horses at the fair but, if he did, that money was missing along with his pocket watch.'

Dempsey was only a couple of yards from them and when he heard mention of the pocket watch he grew afraid. He told Lucinda that he would fill a bag of turf in the haggard for the night's fire. The captain gave him permission to do so but ordered him to come back without delay. Constable Ernest Hudson told Catherine Landricken, a neighbour of the Sly's, to go with Dempsey and help him with the turf. She followed Dempsey. He was ahead of her for a while. There were seven stacks of oats in the haggard. When Dempsey was going past the seventh stack, he took the watch from his pocket, lifted the bottom of a sheaf in the middle of the stack and hid the watch in it. Catherine Landricken saw him tidying the sheaf and she knew that he had hidden some-thing there.

Captain Battersby ordered Lucinda and some of the neighbours into the house as he couldn't continue with his investigations because of the large crowd that was congregating. Many had travelled some distance out of curiosity and there were newspaper reporters there too. The captain knew that rumours would spread without foundation from such a gathering.

'All I want in the house,' he told them, 'are those who were present here at first this morning.'

Although Thomas Singleton had no part to play in the investigation, he went into the house with the others as it was his mother who was being questioned by the captain.

'If you don't know that your husband had a gun,' the captain addressed Lucinda, 'we will have to search the house and sheds.'

On hearing this, Singleton spoke.

'He had a gun,' he said, 'and I know that he wasn't carrying it last night as I had a drink with him.'

He told the captain that Walter took off his coat while he was drinking with him and that he had mentioned that the gun was at home. Singleton had always been concerned that somebody would steal the gun from his coat.

'Where in the house do you think he would hide it?' the captain asked.

Singleton looked at his mother.

'It was in a wooden box he bought with the gun,' he offered. 'Look under the bed.'

Lucinda turned the colour of death and she almost fell to the ground.

Captain Battersby was looking at Lucinda and he became suspicious when he saw Dempsey standing beside her and propping her up. He told Constable Hudson to go to the room and look under the bed. Hudson had gone only a minute when he spoke from the room. He had found the wooden box. He gave it to the captain.

'There is a key for this. Have you any idea, my good woman, where your husband used to keep it?' he continued, knowing that Lucinda was under pressure.

'I know nothing about a key,' she answered boldly.

The captain was growing impatient by this time. He knew that Lucinda was becoming anxious and the servant boy was no better. He looked from person to person around the kitchen.

'The neighbours can go home now,' he said. 'You will be called to the barracks in a few days to make your statements about this morning's events. Go now and thank you for your help on this tragic occasion.'

Even though they would have preferred to see what was to come, the neighbours went out the door in ones and twos.

When there was nobody left in the kitchen but Lucinda Sly, John Dempsey, Singleton, Constable Hudson and himself, Captain Battersby looked straight at Lucinda.

'Give me the key, my good woman,' he demanded.

'Look,' Singleton offered, 'I have a key to the box in the barracks in Bilboa. Walter Sly gave it to me when he bought the gun.'

'I would say that Lucinda has a key,' the captain said taking hold of Lucinda and searching her.

He took a small key out of Lucinda's apron pocket and gave it to Hudson.

'Try this,' he said with a satisfied grin on his face.

Hudson put the key in the lock and opened the box.

'Examine the gun and see if it has been fired recently,' the captain ordered.

'It isn't long since this gun was fired,' Hudson replied, 'and whoever put the bullet back into the gun didn't do it properly.'

'That is what I need,' the captain declared.

He knew immediately that it was one of the two people who lived in the house who had murdered Walter Sly.

'We will have to finish this investigation in the police barracks as this case is very clear and an attorney will have to be present before we can proceed any further,' the captain said.

In the following few days the police collected all the evidence they needed in order to charge a person, or persons, with the murder of Walter Sly. They waited until the funeral was over on the Tuesday, 11 November, before they arrested anybody for the crime.

Lucinda Sly and John Dempsey were walking out of the graveyard when two policemen in plain clothes came up to them. They identified themselves outside the graveyard gate and directed them to a coach that was waiting. The crowd stood outside the graveyard staring at Lucinda and Dempsey being escorted into the coach. They were taken to Carlow town where they were charged with the murder of Walter Sly and locked up in two cells.

In the weeks that followed the murder, every kind of rumour was doing the rounds of the neighbouring parishes. Nothing like this had happened in Carlow in living memory. Everybody had their own version and the story grew with the telling until it was said that Lucinda was a witch who lured her simple servant boy into helping her to murder Walter Sly.

The Crown was not satisfied that the police had a strong enough case yet. A day didn't pass that Captain Battersby didn't visit Lucinda in her cell to break her so that the police would have a clear case to put before the judge.

One day he said to Lucinda, 'John Dempsey has admitted that you two murdered your husband. We have enough evidence to charge both you and Dempsey. As well as that he has said that the two of you had been planning the deed for a month and you were only waiting for the right moment. He admitted that Sly came home from the fair drunk and that one of you hit him on the head. Then, in case he wasn't dead, you put a bullet in his brain with his own gun. You should admit it to me here, then before the minister that you did the deed. God will forgive you and you will go straight up to heaven. John Dempsey has confessed to the priest. His soul is clean before God. Do the same thing and the two of you will be together in heaven.'

But Lucinda was taking no notice of him. Battersby understood eventually that she had lost her mind because the policeman who was guarding her told him that she spent most of the day talking gibberish to herself.

Even the day before the trial began, the minister visited her but she paid no attention to him only to tell him that Walter Sly was a blackguard. 'Yes, go home and do what your husband tells you,' she said. Then she turned her face to the wall.

When Captain Battersby had finished with Lucinda, he questioned John Dempsey again. He admitted that he and Lucinda had killed Sly with his own gun. He wanted to beg God's forgiveness so that he would go to heaven. He had said the same thing, word for word, to the priest who visited him. He even made his confession to prepare his soul to go before God.

By the time the Crown was ready to try the case, the poor woman had already been tried and hanged by the people.

# Chapter Eleven

The Crown fixed the date for the trial of Lucinda Sly and John Dempsey for 16 March, 1835. It was to be held in Deighton Hall in Carlow town. From the day they were arrested it was the event most spoken of among the common people since the coming of Cromwell. It was written about in the national papers and it was the topic of conversation at all the fairs and outside the churches both Catholic and Protestant all over Ireland with every farmer, tailor and tinker adding to it. It was no wonder, then, that early on the morning of 16 March all the roads leading to Carlow town were black with people, some of them on foot, more on horseback and the rich people in coaches, all of them traveling to Deighton Hall to see the witch and the servant boy who murdered a poor farmer cruelly and without pity. Since the murder took place four months earlier there were so many rumours going about that it would have been difficult to separate the truth from the lies that were told about the couple by windbags who had nothing better to do.

At eleven o'clock on the morning of 16 March, the clerk

opened the doors of Deighton Hall for the trial of Lucinda and Dempsey. The space outside the hall was overflowing with ordinary people from all over.

As soon as the officers of the court and the judge were inside the courtroom, the constable who was standing at the door let in some of the crowd. When he thought that enough people were inside, he closed the door.

When the judge was seated, the clerk of the court read the charges that were to be brought against Lucinda Sly and John Dempsey and the attorneys questioned the members of the Grand Jury and the Petit Jury. When both sides were satisfied, every member of the jury swore on the Bible that they would listen carefully and give a verdict without favour. The Petit Jury was put into its own box. Landlords and wealthy farmers who were well known among the important people of Carlow sat on both juries. All of them were men and there wasn't one Catholic among them.

The trial of Lucinda Sly and John Dempsey would be a different matter in the eyes of the Crown. Lucinda was a Protestant and Dempsey was a Catholic. In the eyes of the common people of Carlow, Lucinda was a kind of witch but this was not said officially. The case that the Crown was to put before the court was that Lucinda Sly and John Dempsey had conspired to murder Walter Sly and that they had had sexual relations while she was married to Sly. This was very serious at that time particularly when it resulted in murder. The Crown would put the case before the court that they conspired to murder Walter Sly and that they planned to live together afterwards.

The judge spoke to the jurors before the prisoners were brought in. He told them to listen carefully to the evidence, not to talk to anybody but through the bench; if they weren't clear about a question or answer, they were to let him know and he would seek clarification.

The two prisoners were brought into the court. The crowd who were in the courtroom began to scream and shout at them. The judge brought down his gavel on the bench and threatened to clear the court if the crowd did not stop shouting.

'Everybody who comes before the court has a right to a fair trial,' he said in annoyance. 'A person is not guilty until a guilty verdict has been brought before the judge.'

Lucinda was trembling in her shoes, she was as white as a sheet and she looked as if she were about to faint. Even though Dempsey was afraid, he didn't show it as much as Lucinda. They both swore on the Bible that they would tell the truth. Dempsey walked to his seat. Lucinda sat in the chair beside him with her head down.

The attorney, Seeds was to put the case for the Crown and defending Lucinda and Dempsey was their attorney, Job L. Campion – both Protestants. Dempsey assumed that he wouldn't be treated fairly as he was a Catholic. The Penal Laws were still in force.

The court clerk stated that everything was in order and that the trial could proceed.

Frances Campbell was the first witness. She told the court about Saturday, 18 November, 1834. She said that she left the Carlow Fair with Walter Sly and a neighbour named Ned Radwell.

The three were on horseback. When the attorney for the Crown questioned her as to whether Walter Sly was drunk on that night, she replied that both Sly and Radwell had had a lot to drink but that was not unusual. This always happened with men on fair days, she said. She further testified that on the road home the three of them stopped in Bilboa and went into a tavern to have a drink before they parted and went their separate ways. In the tavern Sly was talking to a man named Thomas Singleton, Lucinda's son by her first marriage, and he introduced him to Radwell and herself. When the attorney for the Crown asked her what kind of man Walter Sly was, she had no hesitation in answering:

'He was a contrary, unscrupulous, bold man who would tear the head from an enemy or anybody who tried to separate him from his property; a person who was not too contented in his mind but, that said, he was always mannerly towards me. He often told me that he had a few enemies, in particular the Brennans, a family he evicted from the land they had rented from him.'

The counsel for the defence had only one question for her.

'Is it true,' he demanded, 'that there once was more than friendship between you?'

She jumped to her feet.

'There was nothing between Walter Sly and me,' she insisted, 'only that we had to travel the same road home from the fair. I am a married woman and a smart alec from the city like you will not destroy my reputation.'

She demanded that the attorney withdraw his remark, which

he had to do as he was only going on hearsay. She finished her statement:

'When Walter and I parted that night he was ready to go home to Oldleighlin.'

She was discharged from the witness box not too happy in her mind.

According to Dr Thomas Rawson, who was in the box after Frances Campbell, it was he who examined the body of Walter Sly in Oldleighlin on Sunday, 9 November, 1834. He testified that a bullet had been fired at Sly's head and that it had come out at the other side. He let the court know that the person who fired the shot would need to have been very close to Sly and that the bullet was the cause of his death even though there were a few other marks on his head as well. Campion did not cross-examine him. Following a few other questions from the attorney for the Crown, the doctor was discharged from the witness box.

Ben Stacey, the Slys' nearest neighbour in Oldleighlin, was called next. He wasn't too happy with the long walk from his chair at the back of the courtroom up to the witness box beside the judge. He was sworn in. Apart from Lucinda Sly and John Dempsey, he was the first to have seen Walter Sly's body. Seeds asked him to tell the court about that morning's events in his own words.

He began: 'I saw the body five or six yards from the stable door and the door of the house was six or seven yards on the other side. Lucinda Sly told me that she had heard her husband's horse coming into the haggard and, shortly after that, she heard another horse coming after him at speed. She heard a shot and a thud as if something heavy had hit the ground. Then a couple of shots were fired at the door and anybody who would come outside the house before morning was threatened with death.'

'It is peculiar,' Seeds observed, 'that no trace of those bullets was found in the wall of the house. But, pray, continue.'

'Lucinda was crying when she told me,' Stacey continued. 'She told me to search Sly's pockets because she thought he should be carrying a large sum of money as he had sold two yearlings at the fair. When there was nothing in his pockets she told me to search his waistcoat for his pocket watch which was very valuable. But there was neither a watch nor chain in his waistcoat.'

Before Stacey left the witness box, he answered a few more questions for the Crown.

'Some of his moustache was singed by the bullet and the side of his head was black . . .'

And, 'He was a comfortable farmer with a reasonably large holding . . .'

The attorney asked him if he had ever seen Walter Sly with a gun.

'I never saw him with a gun,' Stacey answered, 'but it was said that he had bought one as he had many enemies. Trouble follows anybody who has land for rent nowadays. If it isn't the Whiteboys looking for revenge on behalf of the small farmers, it is the horse buyers complaining about a bad animal you have sold them.'

Campion didn't question Stacey as he felt that he had done little to damage his case.

Four more witnesses were called but the Crown's case was not completed yet by Seeds. The clerk of the court called Catherine Landricken, another neighbour of the Slys.

She was not long giving evidence when the case turned tragically against Lucinda and Dempsey. She testified that she had seen Dempsey pulling a sheaf of oats from the stack that was furthest from the stable and putting it back in its place. She became suspicious and informed the police. A policeman named Joseph Flanagan found Walter Sly's watch in the stack on 10 November, she said. When Flanagan was put in the witness box a doubt was put in the jurors' minds when he answered a question Campion put to him concerning the watch. He informed the court that two men were helping him to search the stack in Sly's haggard – Tobin and Brennan. It was Tobin who found the watch in the stack, he said. It was only afterwards he found out that Sly had evicted Brennan from his holding a few years previously.

Flanagan's evidence put another twist in the story because there had been bad blood between Sly and Brennan. Some of the jurors had a different opinion, particularly those who thought that they knew beforehand that Lucinda and Dempsey had murdered Sly. The attorney for the Crown was not pleased and, without more comprehensive evidence, he felt that the two would go free on some technicality or other.

One thing was certain – Walter Sly and the local police knew each other very well and were friendly towards each other. A couple of weeks before the Carlow Fair, John James, a policeman, had gone to Sly's farm to kill a pig. When he was cross-examined, he testified that on the day of the pig killing he saw Lucinda and Dempsey touching hands behind her husband's back. That left the jury in no doubt that there was a sexual relationship between them. But it was pointed out to the attorney for the Crown that more evidence was needed in relation to the murder. If so, they would be depending very heavily on the two witnesses who were yet to appear. These were Bridget Massey and Michael Connors, both neighbours of the Slys.

Bridget Massey and her husband were living two fields above the Slys. They were of the tinker tribe but they had their own little house by this time. Bridget told the court that she knew the Slys very well. She said that they had a stormy relationship from the time they first got married.

'Many times Lucinda told me about the lashings of the horse's whip she got from Walter,' Bridget informed the court. 'When we were cutting the turf last summer she showed me the marks on her back she got from Walter's whip.'

She said that she also knew the servant boy, John Dempsey. Sly had hired him as there was no girl available at the time. One evening when she visited Sly's house she came upon Lucinda and Dempsey in the bedroom together. When the attorney questioned her as to what she thought they were doing in the bedroom she looked at him as if it were a simpleton who put the question to her. She continued with her evidence without answering his question as everybody in the court knew the answer. She said that she often saw Lucinda with her arms around Dempsey's neck. She said she saw things happening that she couldn't describe before a crowd of people when the two of them were digging a meal of potatoes in the field. As she put it, 'The learned man can take a hint.'

Bridget also testified that Lucinda visited her the day that a man named Potts was killed in a quarry on the other side of Carlow town. It was Lucinda who told her the news.

'"Did you hear about a man named Potts who was killed in the quarry yesterday?" Lucinda said to me,' Bridget reported. '"I did not," I replied. "It is a pity it wasn't Walter who was killed," Lucinda remarked, "because if any man deserves to be killed, it is him."'

'Another morning,' Bridget continued, 'Lucinda came to my door asking me to go gathering potatoes. While I was getting ready to go with her, she saw rat poison on the settle. She asked me to give her some of the poison but I asked her had she any rats. Lucinda told me that she had one big rat, Walter, in the bed with her and that she would give him the poison.'

Seeds instructed her to tell the court what time of year it was when that happened.

'It was last October,' Bridget replied.

Then John Dempsey was put into the witness box.

It took the attorney for the Crown only ten minutes to get him talking. Dempsey blurted out exactly how they had murdered Sly. He said he would have to make his peace with God as he couldn't go to his death with such a grave sin on his soul. Lucinda fell in a weakness listening to him. From that moment on, the beatings and whippings she received from Sly from the day they married were of no account. The attorney said that he wouldn't put Lucinda in the witness box as he felt that the case was lost.

The court was adjourned until eleven o'clock the following morning. Michael Connors was yet to be questioned as was Captain James Battersby, the County Inspector. Michael Connors gave his evidence precisely. He stated that he could neither read nor write and that there were a few times in his life that he had hard words with Walter Sly, but that the thing that most upset him was the evening he was eating supper in Sly's house after spending the day working for him. It happened that Sly was away at a fair and Dempsey was milking the cows.

'While we were eating a bite of food,' he began, 'Lucinda let me know that she was half killed by Walter and that he was forever threatening that he would take her name from his will and leave her with nothing. She told me that if I could take Sly from this life that I would get a couple of acres and that I would have the land I was renting free from rent as long as she lived. I told her to shut up immediately and that I would pretend I hadn't heard a word.'

'It wasn't long afterwards,' he continued, 'that I met Dempsey on a fair day in Carlow town. I had a drink with him and he told me I was only a stump of a fool not to have taken up Lucinda's offer . . . Some time later, I was helping Walter to move a horse from one part of his land down to the bog. I told him that it didn't look right that his wife and John Dempsey were so fond of each other. A fortnight after that he met me in a tavern in Carlow town. He had a few in. He told me off for spreading lies about his wife. While he was insulting me he raised his whip over my head. I caught the whip and wrapped it around his neck and told him not to do such a thing again. After that he was as friendly with me as a cow in a cock of hay. I worked for Walter and Lucinda a day here and a day there after that but I minded my own business. If I saw her naked in bed with a man, I kept my mouth shut. Hunger is the best sauce, your honour.'

When James Battersby went into the witness box every eye in the room was on him. He was the one who had gathered all the evidence from Sunday, 9 November until the trial began. He would not be cross-examined but would read out a statement before the judge and jury. This is what he read:

'I was present in the village of Oldleighlin near the house where Walter Sly's body was found on Sunday 9 November, 1834 in the haggard five yards from the stable and seven yards from the door of the house. I saw the injury to the side of Walter Sly's head and the hole near it where the bullet entered. I was present when the box in which the gun was kept was found. Lucinda Sly said to me that she had no key for the box and that she did not know what was in it. I found the key in her apron pocket. After the gun had been examined it was established that it had been fired some hours previously as the smell of gunpowder was still fresh. I asked Constable Hudson, who was present, to insert his finger in the barrel of the gun. When he had done that, he showed me the sweat on his finger. I was virtually certain then that the shot that killed Walter Sly was fired from that gun. I looked over at John Dempsey. I realised that he was very edgy when I was staring at him. He informed me that he would tell me the whole story when he made his statement in the barracks. I knew then that it was Dempsey and Lucinda Sly who planned the murder. But when I questioned Dempsey some days later in his cell in Carlow Gaol he said that he had no part in the murder. But I went to him a week later and told him that I thought he was not telling the truth. Dempsey told me the truth in the presence of two attorneys who were with me.'

That strengthened the case for the Crown. Campion said that he had no more witnesses to call for the defence. It would do his case no good if he put Lucinda in the witness box. She was just recovering from the tremor she got when she heard Dempsey's testimony.

Before the judge instructed the jury to retire to the jury room to arrive at a verdict he told them about their grave responsibility.

Lucinda Sly and John Dempsey were before the court and had not yet been found guilty. The Crown was depending on them to consider the evidence dispassionately. He instructed them to go into the back room and not to come before him until they had reached a verdict.

The jury spent four hours discussing the evidence. They would be close to a decision when one of them would come up with another question and so on until in the end they reached a verdict.

An unnatural silence descended on the courtroom as the jurors took their seats. Every eye was on them.

'Have you reached a verdict in the case of the Crown versus Lucinda Sly and John Dempsey?' the judge asked them.

The foreman of the jury stood.

'We have reached a verdict, your honour,' he began. 'In the case of the Crown versus Lucinda Sly, we find Lucinda Sly guilty of the murder of Walter Sly. In the case of the Crown versus John Dempsey, we find John Dempsey guilty of murder.'

The judge looked at the two of them. He put on his black cap.

'Lucinda Sly,' he spoke in a grave tone, 'it is the judgement of this court that on the 30th of March at half past two in the afternoon outside Carlow Gaol you will be hanged by the neck until you are dead. May God have mercy on your soul.'

When the crowd in the courtroom heard this, they cheered. Lucinda fell in a weakness for a second time. Then the judge brought his gavel down on the bench.

'Silence in court,' he ordered. 'Now, John Dempsey,' he continued, 'on the same date, at the same time and in the same place, you will be hanged by the neck until you are dead. May God have mercy on your soul.'

On 30 March the sky was clear with not a cloud to be seen. There was a cold, light breeze blowing from the north with a harsh streak to it. Crowds were gathering from early morning in the space before the Gaol. It was a big day in town. It wasn't every day that two criminals were hanged.

Everybody wanted to be present and to have the best view when the trapdoor beneath their feet was sprung and they were hanging, their feet shaking for their sins until the life was gone from their bodies.

The gaol door opened and a Protestant minister and a Catholic priest walked out with four policemen escorting the two prisoners. Lucinda appeared weak and drawn but Dempsey walked out the door with his head held high like a man who was ready to go before God. He had made his confession to the priest a few days earlier and had told the authorities – and had admitted in court – that Lucinda and he had planned the murder of Walter Sly and that it was they who had murdered him. Lucinda had not admitted that she had any part in the murder. A column of the British army and a large group of police were present in case there was any trouble during the hanging.

There were steps leading up to the gallows. The ropes were put around the prisoners' necks. The minister and one of the policemen had to keep Lucinda standing while the hangman was putting the rope around her neck. The crowd stood there baying for blood.

'Hang the witch! Hang the two of them!' they shouted.

Dempsey made an attempt to speak to the crowd but they were calling for his and Lucinda's blood and nobody heard him.

'Hang them! Hang them!' they shouted.

The trapdoors were sprung at the same time. Within a few minutes, they were dead.

# Envoi

The old man who had sat beside me every evening for a fortnight turned towards me; he had the same woollen hat on him that he was wearing the first evening I met him in Carlow town.

'It is a fortnight since we met,' he began. 'That is the story of Lucinda Sly and John Dempsey. She is the last woman who was hanged in Carlow town or county but, do you know, I don't think she is satisfied in eternity because – do you see that shop in the place where she was convicted and hanged? It was there the court that convicted Lucinda and Dempsey was convened in 1835. I don't think she is happy in the place she went to after she was hanged and perhaps she is not in heaven yet. People see her ghost from time to time and strange things happen in the dead of night in the restaurant and in the shop. There are people who say that her spirit is haunting the place waiting for release from this world.'

I looked at the old man.

'Don't tell me you believe in ghosts,' I said.

'Oh, I believe strongly in them,' he assured me. 'Not only that, but maybe it is I who will make the connection. Have you finished your work here in Carlow?' he enquired.

'I'm going home tomorrow,' I told him.

'My work isn't finished yet,' he said, rising from his seat. He began to walk towards the grocer shop.

He was just out of sight inside the shop when an important question struck me. I went after him into the shop. I looked all around but there was no sight of the old man. The attendant was looking at me expecting me to buy something.

'Where did the old man who came in just before me go?' I asked him.

He looked at me.

'You are the first customer that came in the door in half an hour,' he said.

I looked around again. The attendant looked at me carefully.

'Are you the man,' he enquired, 'who was sitting on the seat out there every evening for the last fortnight writing in a copybook?'

'I am,' I told him, 'and the old man I am looking for was sitting beside me.'

The attendant stood there still staring at me.

'I saw no old man beside you,' he spoke in disbelief, 'but a few times I passed the seat I thought I heard you talking gibberish to yourself.'

I didn't say another word but walked out the door.

I am constantly wondering since then about the man with the

woollen hat. Was he from this world or was he sent from the other world to somehow help Lucinda Sly?

I set this down exactly as the old man told me and, no matter what the shopkeeper said, it is he who told me about the events in Oldleighlin.